Elvira Totterheels in Gran Canaria

MännerschwarmVerlag

Elvira Klöppelschuh

# Elvira Totterheels
# in Gran Canaria

Sea, Sun, Sand and

a New Pair of Shoes!

Translated and Adapted for English Readers
by Ashley Lancaster

Männerschwarm Verlag
Hamburg 2015

Original German title: Elvira auf Gran Canaria
© Männerschwarm Verlag, Hamburg 2006

Bibliografische Information der Deutschen Bibliothek
Die Deutsche Bibliothek verzeichnet die Publikation
in der Deutschen Nationalbibliografie; detaillierte
bibliografische Daten sind im Internet über
http://dnb.ddb.de abrufbar.

Elvira Klöppelschuh
Elvira Totterheels in Gran Canaria
Translated and adapted for English readers by Ashley Lancaster

© Männerschwarm Verlag, Hamburg 2015
© English translation by Ashley Lancaster, 2001

Cover design: Carsten Kudlik, Bremen
Graphic Artwork by Ralf König
Printed by Finidr s.r.o, (Czech Republik)
1. Print run 2015
ISBN of print edition 978-3-86300-204-6
ISBN of eBook 978-3-86300-207-7

Männerschwarm Verlag
Steindamm 105 – 20099 Hamburg
www.maennerschwarm.de

### Are all the hatboxes on board?
### Off on hols from Blighty to Playa del Ingles
### Or: didn't Nefertiti have a charwoman then?

I'm really not superstitious, but when Brenda, my very, very best friend in the whole wide world, plans to travel down from Preston to London on Friday the thirteenth then it's just highly improbable that nothing'll go wrong! Either she'll leap up from 'er seat on an irresistible impulse and pull the emergency cord just outside Wigan because she's just realised she left her favourite chapeau on the platform, or she'll get on the wrong train, go in the completely wrong direction and end up in Glasgow, wondering why I'm not there to pick her up and why (having nodded off in the compartment and dreamt of rippling, bronzed, Spanish hunks) the locals are all a pale blue colour and even the naffs are wearing skirts in rather quaint olde worlde tartan patterns!

Usually Brenda is an utterly reliable thing. When she says, «I'm coming», then generally she comes! She just gets a bit flustered at times. Especially when she's been flitting around at work like a humming bird on acid and is totally knackered. And that's exactly why we flew off on our hols to Gran Canaria. For four whole weeks!

In case you're wondering why we call her Brenda, when in fact she was actually christened Brendan, (after some sporting type who apparently won lots and lots of prizes for running around and jumping over things, or something like that), it all has to do with milk shakes. You see, Brenda is a real whizz in the kitchen and works absolute wonders with a blender. Her milk shakes are famous right across the north west. Hence: Brenda's Blender!

Because I know Brenda and the chaos that is her life only too well, I made a special point of calling up our mutual girlfriend Molly (because when I met her she was off her trolley!) in Preston and said: «Dearest Molly, please do us a huge favour luvvie and see to it that your Auntie Brenda gets her act together re. holiday plans! Disconnect the phone, hide the voddy, make sure she packs her passport, plastic, keys for the apartment in Playa, electric razor and Christmas pud, and don't let her out of your sight until she's on that train and it's pulling out of the station!»

«Right you are,» says Molly, «I will. And what about the plane tickets, shouldn't I remind her about them an' all?»

«Don't even think about it! Otherwise she'll get completely hysterical and turn the entire flat upside down looking for them. I've got the tickets here.»

«All right then, that's okay,» said Molly, but of course, as it turned out, nothing was okay!

So there I was on Friday the thirteenth of December in the madding crowds at Euston station like a pearl among swine (I was premiering this catchy little red ensemble I had snapped up from a boutique off the King's Road the day before – far beyond my means if I'm honest, next month's rent will be late again, but a girl has to get her priorities right!) and guess who was nowhere to be seen? Brenda, who else?!

I ran around everywhere looking for her; had she gone down into the Tube remembering we'd be taking the Northern Line to my humble abode off Soho Square? No! Had she popped into *W.H.'s* to stock up on *Cosmo* and *Harpers & Queens* for the flight? No! I even ventured into the cottage to see if she had succumbed to one of her irresistible urges again. No! Once I eventually found a phone that worked – I'm sure the main reason for having those phone boxes there is so that illicit local businesses can advertise their services; is there really such a call for French polishing in Central London? – I tried calling Molly to see if she could shed any light on the problem. Unfortunately I only got her answering machine with that infuriating opera music and her shrieking her lungs out with «cheer up if you're all alone, and leave a message after the tone!» to the tune of some wellknown opera that everybody knows from some advert when they were a kid but I certainly couldn't identify; I'm not that sort of queen! For want of anything better to do and to vent at least just a little of my frustration, I screamed «I haaaaaaate opera» at the top of my voice in the best soprano I could muster down the phone and slammed the receiver down. This prompted a few strange looks from passers-by but made me feel quite a bit better for at least two and a half seconds!

After about an hour of semi-panic and visions of Brenda standing all alone like a lost sheep in an enormous floral sun hat on a platform in Glasgow wondering just what had happened, I decided there was nothing more I could do there. So I decided to head home and hope that she'd have the initiative to attempt to make contact via that newfangled gadget, the electric telephone! (Brenda is not hot on technology! She's got the most ancient television set because she kept losing the remote to the new one she'd rented – she got through four in two months before finally giving up and returning it to Radio Rentals. The man was not best pleased! – and anyway she likes fiddling with knobs, she says!!)

As I rounded the corner of my street, what sight should greet my tired eyes but Brenda in an enormous sun hat, plonked down on an enormous suitcase, reigning over a bizarre array of luggage piled up around her.

«Where 'ave you come from?» was all I could gasp out in my surprise.

«From t'station duckie, I got a taxi in the end, since you weren't there to pick uz up! D'ya know, I had to lug this lot all by meself as muggins 'ere naturally had the good luck to hazard upon London's fattest cabby who simply refused to shift his fat arse and 'elp me!»

After we had somehow managed to haul what had to have been everything she owned up to my third floor flat (I'm sure I heard the kitchen sink clanking in one of those bags!), with me frantically wracking my brains for ideas as to how I could persuade her to leave at least 90% of it at home, the puzzle was solved as to what had happened. On one of her irresistible urges Brenda had, at the last minute, persuaded Molly to drive her across to Leeds to pick up this «simply fabulous pair of shoes» that she had seen the week before but for some reason had not bought and «just had to have for the hols», and had taken the train down from there. Of course it didn't occur to the dozy cow that trains from Leeds come into King's Cross and not Euston as they «only ever have one station per town in the north which makes life so much easier duckie ...» Provincial queens can be so trying at times!!

Having finally got to the bottom of that one (an expression the lovely Brenda can never resist slipping in when she's just managed to seduce the latest man of her dreams), she leapt to her feet, impulsive as ever, and shrieked:

«Elvira, darling, this is an emergency, I simply must have chips! After all this excitement I require nutritious sustenance immediately.»

So off we trolled to the local chippy to drown our sorrows in grease and non-brewed condiment!

Having thus strengthened ourselves, on arriving home I immediately tackled the dilemma of Brenda's excessive luggage.

«But it isn't excessive at all dearest, I only packed the barest essentials, honest!» I tried explaining that airlines have weight limits and if everyone packed that much there'd only be enough room for about six people on the plane. «Well they should get a bigger plane then, sweetie shouldn't they, and besides which I've lost eight pounds in the last six weeks which surely more than makes up for a few cosmetics that weigh absolutely nothing anyway ...» There's no point trying to argue with logic like that at two minutes to midnight on Friday the thirteenth. I only had to wait two more minutes and this day would be over.

«So now that we have sampled the culinary delights of this fabulous metropolis what's next on the agenda? If I'm in London I simply have to let it take advantage of me. Where shall we go, what shall we do, who shall we sweep off their feet and show a good time?»

I held my breath and watched the second hand on the kitchen clock tick painfully slowly up to twelve, and sure enough it was tomorrow. As soon as I pointed out that our flight was at 9 o'clock and that we had to be at Gatwick by 7.30 which meant getting up at the crack of dawn at the very latest, all ideas of merrymaking suddenly evaporated, and with a gasp and some incomprehensible reference to beauty sleep Brenda flitted off to my spare room.

I set all the alarm clocks I could get my hands on, and not being able to bear the thought of having to struggle with all that luggage in the small hours I waited till Brenda was fast asleep and snoring like a juggernaut and simply repacked. Although we do have our little differences from time to time (I would not describe twelve pairs of shoes as the barest essentials) she really is a jewel!

Having stashed the excess I hit the sack myself but just could not get to sleep. I don't know what you think about in bed the night before going on your hols. Usually people worry about having forgotten something important. Not me. Not since my girlfriend Varicose Vera gave me this holiday-thingies-checklist (see page 187) which is just so handy. She had this long affair with an accountant and he developed this system for her on a computer.

No, I always ask myself if I've really packed the right things. For example, Brenda mentioned to me that you can't drink the tap water in Playa and so you have to fetch water from somewhere else for making tea or cooking. Where from, I naturally forgot to ask, and had this romantic image of a village well with palm trees and all! I saw something dinky like that in this nature programme about Africa on the telly, and if you look on a map at where Gran Canaria actually is, then it's just left a bit of the Sahara Desert, and the Bedouins that troll about in the desert fetch their water from the well as well. The Bedouins don't actually fetch the water themselves but get their wives, the Bedouwimin, to fetch it! But knowing Brenda she'll refuse point blank to go out on the street dragged up as a Bedouwoman so I'll have to do it!

As I lay there awake in bed I went through all my clothes in my mind's eye and realised to my horror that I didn't have anything suitable for fetching water. Something long and flowing would have been just the job. And to think I could've borrowed something from my girlfriend Stilly (not only due to her favourite shoes but also because it rhymes with silly!) if only I'd've thought of it in time. Yes, and then I could've practised balancing one of them enormous terracotta water pots on my head without it crashing down to the ground, shattering into a million pieces and wasting all that precious water. Those pots aren't cheap you know! But you can start off with a tin pot for beginners can't you? But those are just the sort of things you only ever think of at the last minute and then you just have to wait and see what happens.

«Maybe there's some old curtain or a bed sheet in the house we've rented that could be run up into something fitting in a jiffy,» I thought, and was really looking forward to my first holiday in Gran Canaria.

At 5 o'clock the next morning when all the alarm clocks started buzzing and clanking I felt as though I hadn't slept at all. But when the clock radio went off with Cliff Richard singing, «We're all goin' on a summer holiday, doin' things we always wanted to …» (and I can imagine just what things too!) I suddenly felt fabulous again.

After what she insisted was a traditional Lancashire breakfast (a pot of tea and twenty ciggies), darling Brenda was in such good spirits, bless 'er heart, she didn't even notice most of her luggage had gone walkies. Thrilled at the prospect of four full weeks of sea, sun, sand and showing off her fabulous new shoes, we set off for Victoria. Brenda, whose first sexual experience had been an encounter with a ticket collector at Lancaster station that had left her with a thing about British Rail uniforms, was delighted to see yet another station. «So many stations and so little time!» she squealed as we swished from our taxi to the ticket office (some people are so easy to please!).

The first blow to our spirits came when we went to buy our tickets for the Gatwick Express. It's called «Express» not coz it's so quick but coz you need an American Express card to pay for it! Nobody carries that much cash with them these days!

By the time we arrived at Gatwick most of the queue was through and we didn't have to wait long at all until it was our turn. I noticed straight away that the check-in lady was also a friend of Dorothy's. She kept fanning herself with people's tickets as if she was having trouble breathing, and couldn't stop hopping about on her seat like a demented sparrow.

But as is so often the case with these uniform queens, she had no sympathy for her own kind. The baggage allowance was 30 kilos and I really only did have 32 kilos. She didn't have anything against the few grams I was over, but somehow I must have not distributed the weight correctly or something. Then as I put my case and my dinky little beach bag on the conveyor the stupid cow asked:

«Do you have any hand luggage?»

«No,» I answered quite innocently, not having a clue what she was on about, when all of a sudden she slapped one of her sticky labels on my beach bag and off it sailed.

«Stop, stop, bring it back,» I screamed. «Me beach bag, I 'ave to take it on board with me.»

«It weighs nine kilos. It's too heavy.»

«So what? I lugged it all the way 'ere. I'll certainly be able to lug it onto the plane.»

«That's as maybe,» she said fanning herself with our tickets and rolling her eyes all the way back like some faded diva! «But you're only allowed three kilos.» What was I supposed to say to that? Just one of my toilet bags weighed three kilos by itself.

«Listen to me,» I said, «in the last five months I've been on a crash diet and 'ave lost six and a half kilos,» I said calmly. «Does that mean that five months ago you wouldn't 'ave taken me with a three kilo bag, or what?»

«That's not the point. Just check in your beach bag and everything will be fine.»

«Not on your life Missy! It'll get so shaken up I won't be able to find a thing afterwards.»

«Then why don't you just take out what you need for the flight and put it in a plastic bag?»

«I don't think so dear! I'll have you know I've got a Gold Card at Harrods, and you expect me to travel with a *Tesco's* carrier bag. Well really!»

The ridiculous battle of the bags went on for quite a while, and Brenda and I had to confer as to what we should do with my oh-so-important little things. Eventually we had the fabulous idea of simply checking Brenda's bag. The snotty little jumped-up ticket collector agreed to that, Thank God! Of course we put all the important things from Brenda's bag into mine first so hers weighed at least three kilos more. And so we finally managed to get on board the plane all in one piece.

We found our seats pretty much smack in the middle of the plane, right by the gangway in the middle row. So there was no looking out of the window, but at least I could stretch my lallies out a bit.

Brenda dropped right off to sleep and I leafed through one of those duty free mags and had a listen to the radio programme

12

that they always have coming out of the armrest. Then I re-clined my seat back as far as it would go (about three and a half inches by the feel of it) and tried to sleep a bit.

Unfortunately though I couldn't get off at all as a man and woman behind me kept rabbiting on. It was so annoying that I just gave in and had to listen to what they were saying. First they went on about Auntie Ethel's Christmas present, and then about what they were going to cook for lunch on Christmas Day. Somehow though they really didn't sound like a normal straight couple.

«I really must take a look at Cynthia,» said the chap all of a sudden.

«No Geoffrey, just let her sleep a bit more!»

«Oh I don't know, do you think she really is asleep? I'd bet-ter just take a quick peek, Mummy.»

SLAP! And then all was quiet!

«Geoffrey's probably just got a clip round the ear off his mummy by the sound of it,» I thought, and just then Brenda came to. She straightened up, glanced around quite noncha-lantly from left to right and whispered to me: «Strange, I can't see any Jessies on here. Do you think we're the only ones?»

Now sometimes Brenda really can be a bit thick. The plane was over half full and the dozy cow hadn't even noticed! In the row in front of us there was a couple, obviously on their honeymoon. They were all over each other all the time, it was so sweet. Two rows further forward on the right were three Marys that I knew by sight from off the scene. And a couple of rows further down on the left were two boys who were just so good-looking they couldn't possibly have been straight. Unfor-tunately I couldn't see any further. Behind us, this much I had realised by now, was at least one more.

«Well, you must be really exhausted,» I said to Brenda. «Or are you sittin' on your ears? 'Ave an earwig to them two behind us.»

And then it went on just as it had started. «We've been flying for two hours now Mummy. Cynthia can't be asleep any more.»

«Can't you just read for a bit or something my boy? Cynthia needs her P and Q too you know.»

«It'll be too hot for her. I'll just take off the rain cape.»

«Leave it!» SLAP! Geoffrey got it again.

«Have they smuggled a stowaway on board or what?» whispered Brenda.

«No,» I said, «that can't be a person.»

«Oh God, not a python?»

«I don't think so, it must be some kind of furry animal.»

«How on earth d'ya know that? Cynthia sounds more like a python to me.»

«Most queens that go on holiday with their mothers don't have pythons with rain capes. They usually have some little doggy or something.»

«In the luggage rack? Are you mad?»

«Have a listen then. Geoffrey's always talking down to the floor.»

Brenda lifted her legs up off the floor just to be on the safe side and peered through them like some deranged rabbit.

«Well, I'm just going to take her cape off now Mummy. It's just far too hot for her otherwise.»

«Well, go on then.»

I felt Geoffrey pushing his head against the back of my seat as he rummaged around with something on the floor. They must have some piece of luggage down there, I thought. Then suddenly I heard a strange squeaking sound.

«I just can't stand it any more. I simply have to take a look,» whispered Brenda, and ogled as unobtrusively as possible backwards over the seat.

«Well, what is it then?» I asked on tenterhooks.

«A long-legged white rat.»

«I don't believe it, that's against quarantine regulations.»

«It is. A small white creature with fur.»

«Come off it. I'm sure it's a doggy. Probably one o' them chee-wow-wows or whatever they're called. They're very fashionable at the moment.»

«I'm sure the little thing's handy, but it's as ugly as sin!»

«Who? Geoffrey?»

«No, the doggy.«

Behind us there was a rustling and then Geoffrey said: «There my darling, but now you have to go back to bed. Soon we'll be in Playa and then we'll go to the beach for a swim. Or would you rather stay up a bit now?»

«Now put her back in her basket. People are looking.» That was the mother.

«Basket? That's not a basket, it's a customised vanity case with iron bars on the front.»

«What does Geoffrey look like then?» I asked.

«Like a naff, just a bit more queeny.»

«And the mother?»

«Like Mrs. Slocombe.»

«Well, I think it's nice that they're going on holiday together.»

«Oh I don't know,» said Brenda. «It can be hell on earth.»

«Oh I think you're being too severe.»

Then we had a really good long chat about how it is with queens and their mothers, and all in all somehow the hours on the flight just flew by.

Around about lunch time we landed at the airport in Gran Canaria. We got there so quickly that by the time we arrived we didn't even have to put our watches back! It took an absolute age till our cases finally came trollin' down the conveyor belt. I was beginning to think the dizzy ticket collector had sent 'em off on a tugboat from Docklands. But the waiting around did have its good side coz all of a sudden two blokes came up and spoke to us.

«Are you goin' to Playa?»

«Yeah, straight to Playa.»

«Us too. We can go together and share the taxi if you like.»

«Yeah,» piped up Brenda, «that'd save us all a bob or two.»

Once the last hat box had finally turned up we got a taxi straight away and set off. The weather was absolutely fabulous. At least 25 degrees and a very pleasant little breezette that made me feel like a completely new woman!

But what I saw next really was very disappointing. Wherever you looked there was only this horrid grey gravel lying all about. Nothing green as far as the eye could see as we drove down the motorway through this barren lunar landscape. To the left, ever so far away, was the blue sea, and to the right in the distance only barren, dried out stony mountains. Every now and again you could see a few little groups of shacks thrown together and long rows of plastic sheeting under which the natives were presumably hiding something. But, as I found out later, they were only tomato fields.

To be honest, the very thought of spending the hols in all this gravel wasn't exactly thrilling. In the brochures it really had looked very different.

After we'd been hacking it down the motorway for quite a while we suddenly came to an enormous sign in front of a gravel slope saying «Sioux City».

«Do they make cowboy films here or what?» I asked Brenda.

«No, that's a kind of western theme park where the naffs can go and play cops and robbers or something,» she said.

«They built that for the tourists,» said one of the blokes from the airport, «so we can recover from the hard life on the beach!»

«Well I think it's all terribly bleak here,» I said completely frustrated. «Where are all the white beaches and the palm trees?»

»There's a little while to go yet.»

Then we drove up onto a sort of mountain and through a sharp right hand bend and suddenly everything completely changed.

«That's San Agustin and it leads straight into Playa del Ingles and Maspalomas,» Brenda explained.

As I saw it I couldn't believe my eyes. In the middle of this gravel desert they'd thrown up a tourist resort right by the sea.

«That looks like a council estate in the East End!» I exclaimed most disappointed.

«Well that's just the way it is here. But at least you can swim and enjoy the sun the whole year round.»

Everywhere there were modern blocks of flats and terraced houses on the streets with complexes of fenced-in bungalows in between. And naturally loads of restaurants and bars and shops along the Avenidas. I couldn't see anything typically Spanish at all, except of course for the gardens with lots of foreign trees and bushes growing in them. If it hadn't've been for the greenery and if the sun hadn't been shining so fabulously I think I would've screamed. And then I suddenly realised that the whole town seemed strangely empty.

«Everybody's down at the beach now, tryin' to get a suntan,» Brenda explained.

«Oh yes o' course, that's why we're here isn't it?»

The two that shared the taxi with us were staying in a kind of round high tower block called Hotel *Waikiki*. So we dropped them off there and they gave us 1,500 pesetas as the whole journey had cost about 3,000.

Then it didn't take long till we came to the *Europlaya Club*. It was directly on Avenida de Tirajana, which is the main drag in Playa where the traffic thunders up and down. And that's where we were staying. Two rows of little square housettes with tidy little gardens. The whole complex looked really cosy. Our house was on the right-hand side in the second row and – Thank God! – we couldn't hear the noise from the street at all.

And then all of a sudden I was really enthralled: a garden with a lawn and fantastic palm trees and cacti, red hibiscus flowers, oleander and then a sort of flowering purple grass that was called bougainvilla or something like that, and genuine strelitzia and everywhere in between some other gay bushy stuff. A really pretty little wild garden with a hammock in it and with sun loungers. The whole thing was surrounded by a vine-covered wall so no one could see in.

«Well, now what d'ya reckon?» Brenda asked.

«I never said a word!» I said. «It's absolutely fabulous!»

The house was just as good, and fabulously furnished. Everything a girl could possibly want. From a hair dryer to an iron and great big fluffy white bath towels. And when Brenda inspected the kitchen she just couldn't stop squealing «fabulous, fabulous ... !»

«Shall I cook something?» she called out.

«Is there anything in the fridge then?»

«No, just a bottle of sparkling wine.»

«Great, well let's cook that then.»

So we drank the wine while we unpacked our things. The bedrooms were on the first floor. Of course Brenda nabbed the one with the TV and the video in it for herself didn't she. Typical! But downstairs in the living room there was another one, and as I started to fiddle about with it I noticed there was a Bette Davis film in it. It was the one where Bette plays Charlotte and gets so terrorised by her wicked sister that in the end she does both her and her lover in with a large flower pot over the head. Well, that scene where Bette's standing on the balcony, drops the pot on their heads and opens her eyes really wide in glee, that we had to watch three times. Somehow that really got us in the mood for Playa, we decided. Then I had to have a quick lie down for half an hour. At about half past four Brenda suddenly appeared in my room all impatient and woke me up.

«We must get going now or *Marlene's* will be as dead as a dodo,» she said, and already had her summery outfit on.

So I just had a quick shower and freshened up my hair with the hair dryer so it looked all bouncy and natural again.

Then we shot down the Avenida and soon came to a shopping centre that was called *La Cita* and was a total maze. You have to keep going up and down stairs all the time and round dozens of corners, and I was simply amazed that Brenda could find her way through all the confusion of little alleys. Somehow they all looked the same. One boutique after another, and each hardly bigger than a shoe box. There were those ghastly shiny tracksuits hanging all over the place and I was just thinking to myself: «Who actually buys this load of old cat shit?» when suddenly Brenda cried out: «Here we are.»

Well, *Café Marlene* is one of those slightly larger shoe boxes without walls on three sides so that you sit under a roof in the alley and can have a really good look at everything that flits by.

First of all we ordered coffee with brandy to celebrate our arrival. And just as I was having a good peek round to see who was there, suddenly this really good-looking guy sat down a couple of tables away from us, unfortunately not alone.

Just as I was having a closer look at the guy, both of them smiled sweetly over at us.

«Well that's a fine start,» I thought, and felt really good.

But not for long. You see the other one was smiling back much more than the really good-looking guy. So I decided to hold back a bit until I could judge the situation better. Unfortunately it didn't improve. After a while the good-looking boy stopped looking over. His mate though couldn't stop.

I didn't want to be impolite on the first day though, so every now and then I grinned over at him for the sake of etiquette and just chatted with Brenda.

And so the time passed and I didn't think of the dishy guy any more until suddenly they stood up and both went off in separate directions. But just as I threw a last look after the good-looking one, the other one was suddenly right in front of me and said:

«Will I see you at *Yumbo* tonight then?»

«Sure,» I said in the butchest voice I could muster.

«Great,» he replied, and with that he was gone.

Brenda had already started drumming her fingers on her temples (she always does that when she's nervous) and said, «I just don't believe it.»

I think it's a great feeling when someone tries to chat you up. At least it proves you're still in demand. After all, it would be really daft to spend the whole holiday sittin' around in pubs if not a soul showed the blindest bit of interest.

But of course it's always a little tricky if you're out and about with your best girlfriend.

Now there's never been anything between Brenda and myself. That's why we have such a relaxed relationship with each other. But a little competitive jealousy does rear its ugly little head from time to time.

«Do you really want to meet that gentleman later on at *Yumbo*?» she asked with just the tiniest touch of sarcasm.

«I don't even know what *Yumbo* is. What kind of a place is it?»

«It's another shopping centre like *Cita*.»

«What, another maze?»

«No, *Yumbo* looks somehow sort of Roman, with different levels and little columns all over the place.»

«And that's why the girls all go running off there at night or what?»

«Not coz o' the columns. Because of all the gay bars that are there.»

«Oh, so that's why we're staying directly opposite *Yumbo*.»

«O' course. You don't think I'd stay out in the sticks somewhere and 'ave to trek miles and miles every night like some madwoman just to go to some nelly bar do ya? In Playa everything is really well organised anyway. After breakfast everyone goes to the beach. And after the beach everyone comes straight here to *Marlene's*.»

«Straight here? With beach bags and without doing their hair?»

«O' course, it's really relaxed here. That goes on until about six o'clock, and then more and more naffs start coming in.»

«And where does everyone go after that?»

«After *Marlene* everyone runs home an' freshens up. That takes a little while doesn't it? Then ya go out to eat. At about half past ten you have to be in Pub *Nestor* though. That's in the *Yumbo Centre*. And then at eleven thirty at the earliest ya just go up the steps round the corner from *Nestor's* to *Tubos* or *Mykonos*. They're a sort of mixture of bar an' disco. It's really good there for just standing around, chatting and havin' a good vada at everything that flits by.»

«And how long d'ya stay there then?»

«Up till about twelve thirty everyone gathers at *Mykonos*, and then at around one thirty the first start to shoot off into *Metropol*, that's like a real club for dancin'. It's on the same floor just a few metres further along, that goes on till about four. Then it dies a death. If you're still up for it ya can then dash off to *XL* and *Kings Club*. But that's over on the other side, I'll show you that later. Right now I'm simply dyin' o' hunger!»

So then we went off to eat. We ended up in this place where you could stuff yourself stupid for 950 pesetas. I took total advantage of it whereas Brenda, who's always trying to lose weight, just sat peeling prawns for hours. I stuffed myself so full I started to fall asleep. «Now I really need a coffee,» I said, and peered searchingly over to the buffet.

«Oh Bloody Nora!» cried Brenda, and thrust her watch under my nose. It was twenty past ten. «You can't 'ave one, we haven't got time. We 'ave to get to *Nestor's*.»

«Why all the stress? We're on holiday.»

«Yes, it's always like that here.»

So we quickly paid the bill and scurried back up the Avenida to where we lived. From there we only had to scoot across the road and we were in the *Yumbo Centre* and standing in front of *Nestor's*.

«How handy,» I thought, and looked around to see if I could find a couple of free chairs in the throng. Suddenly, just as I was standing there scanning the area like one of those dinky radar thingies on ships, someone screeched into my ear: «Yoo-hoo!»

Well, that really was a surprise. It was Vera from Manchester who I've known for absolutely years (Vera because she is to gin what fish are to water!). She was as brown as a berry, enough to make a girl really jealous.

«My God, you're so brown,» I cried.

«Well, a girl does what a girl can,» she replied. «Why don't ya come an' join us?»

We somehow managed to find a couple of chairs, and as we sat down at the table there was another screech as there sat Gerty (due to a certain habit, she quickly became known in certain circles as Dirty Gerty!) who was one of Vera's discarded spouses, and a couple of very nice-looking numbers – a geriatric nurse from Wolverhampton and a roofer from Palermo.

After we'd all been introduced the first necessity was, of course, to find out who was with who!

«'Ave you two got married again?» I asked Gerty at an opportune moment.

«Not really,» she said, and gazed longingly across at Luigi, the roofer from Palermo. Therefore she must have something goin' with the bloke from Wolverhampton, I thought. Funny, he looked so straight, I was really amazed at what turns out to be gay these days. Apparently though he wasn't properly queer, he just helps out when there's a rush on! Then Gerty explained to me that her real husband was sulking back home in Manchester coz he couldn't get any time off work.

Now this Luigi was a really international number. He looked Italian, but he spoke with such a broad Geordie accent I could hardly understand a word he said, being a proper London girl myself. Obviously spent half his waking hours in the gym coz he had tits that made Brenda's eyes stand out on stalks.

So, as we were just sitting there and chitt-chattin' about the weather and this and that all of a sudden this bloke that Brenda had met on her last holiday came up. Freddie. He was a blacksmith, or at least he claimed to be and sat down next to me.

Then I learned an awful lot about shoein' horses and how different types of horses had different types of hooves. You see Arabian horses generally only need six-inch nails under their feet whereas police horses need eight. In general the horseshoes depend on whether the horse is a steeplechaser, a dressage horse or just some old nag. And when the horse trots about on the street in winter it has to have a special plate inserted between the hoof and the shoe to stop it getting clogged up with mush so the horse doesn't slip up and land on its arse. But then when the horses go out into the fields in summer they put Pirelli shoes on because the ground is soft.

All of this was really totally fascinating, but I thought this business with the Pirelli shoes was a bit odd. Up till then I'd only ever heard of Pirelli tyres. But then maybe Freddie had nailed the odd tyre onto the occasional old nag by accident. Anyway, all of a sudden it was midnight so we didn't hold our horses and galloped up the stairs to *Mykonos*.

*Mykonos* is like two shoe boxes built around a corner with the fronts open. And on the walls there are these kind of chicken ladders which you can sit on and from which you have a good view over all the comings and goings.

I trolled up to the bar to fetch a wee drinkee just as this wrinkled old queen in yachting drag – she looked like she'd just popped over from Henley – ordered her drink in this loud upper class twit voice:

«G and T please,» she boomed, and just in case the Spanish barman didn't understand her she added, «that's a gin and tonic to you, dearie.»

Without batting an eyelid the barman poured the drink and shot back, «Ice and a slice? That's lemon and frozen water to you, dearie!»

I'd just got me voddy when someone tapped me on the shoulder and said: «Hello! Elvira? Is that you?»

Well who did we have here? It was Hakon and Kenneth. This was getting to be a regular reunion. I'd met both of 'em years and years before at a party when Kenneth ran in the London marathon. «Yes,» I said delighted, «yeeees.» You see Kenneth and Hakon were two extremely good-looking policemen from Stockholm. And these two gorgeous Swedes were there with a whole gang. As we were all being introduced I kept looking around to see if that good-looking bloke from *Marlene's* had popped up anywhere. But of course he hadn't, so I passed the time chatting to this Scottish pensioner who was part of the Swedish group.

«So what took you from Scotland to Sweden?» I asked her, thinking it couldn't be that much colder. Maybe she'd been caught having indecent relations with a haggis and had to leave the country in disgrace! I couldn't help grimacing slightly at her extremely daring hotpants which she'd obviously stitched together from the remains of an old pair of jeans.

«I married a Swede.» So she was into vegetables after all!

«What? The full Monty? White dress, in front of an altar with confetti?»

«Och no. Gays can't get prroperly married in Sweden till next yearr or the yearr after. At the moment we'rre still living in sin.»

«What, really in sin?»

«Aye. For more 'an forty years noo. I met me man on thae platform at Glasgow station in 1952. He wanted to go to Sweden too. Since then we've been trravelling together.»

«Great! Every day?»

«Aye, o' course. Arre you married too, hen?»

«No, I'm just on the lookout to see if I can find something.» I quickly looked around again to see if the *Marlene* chap had appeared with his other half.

«Are ye at least havin' a wee holiday rromance, dolly?» the OAP drilled further into my wounds.

«I only just arrived today.»

«Well if I werre yooo I'd at least get mesel' a wee holiday rromance, petal.»

«I fully intend to,» I said, and looked around again.

«That's goood. Particularly in these harrsh times.»

«It's not that easy ya know. How d'ya know that the gorgeous Adonis you've been making eyes at all evening isn't on the last day of his holiday and is gonna shoot off home first thing in the morning? Then the whole palaver would've been a complete waste of time.»

«Oh girrl, herre in Playa therre's a really simple trick to solve that 'un. The white 'uns 've just arrived, the bronze, tanned 'uns could leave any time! It's as simple as that, dolly.»

One really shouldn't underestimate the wisdom of such elderly ladies! I'd never've thought of that all on my own!

«I must say I'm g'tting a wee bit nerrvous too,» exclaimed the OAP all of a sudden. «Where has me hubby got to? He should've been done ages ago.»

«Done? What with?»

«Well, he had to clean the wee bungalow.»

«What, in the middle of the night?»

«Aye petal, yoo see we have our responsibilites. Yoo see all that young meat sitting at that barr yonder? Those are all our wee children. Seven of 'em,» she said, and pointed proudly at the group of Swedes that were sitting at the bar in *Mykonos* and partly in *Tubos* and were knocking it back as fast as they could.

«You have to watch out that they don't fall off their stools I suppose, eh?»

«Aye, that's just it,» said the OAP. «They just can't take it cause the whisky in Scandinavia is sooo expensive. So 'ere they rreally let themselves goo. Then as soon as they get tirred they throw up all o'er the place and we have to crawl around on our hands and knees mopping it all up.»

How practical for the Swedish kiddies to bring along a couple of OAPs for the dirty work, I was just thinking as Brenda flitted up and whispered into my ear: «Look over there, there's your lover boy from *Marlene's*. Don't you want to go over and say hello?»

«Oh, no doubt he'll come over of his own accord,» I said but of course had to look over to see if the cute guy was there too. He was, of course, and of course I then had to look to see if he was looking, which, as at *Marlene's,* he wasn't of course. So I just continued chatting to the Scottish OAP about childcare. She told me exactly what drag she wore on the day of Queen Silvia's coronation, and all these special little tricks she's developed for cleaning windows so as not to leave those really annoying little smears that always stand out a mile as soon as the sun shines on them. She really was such a wealth of knowledge!

The first thing I had to do though was look over to see what colour the chap from *Marlene's* was. Well, he was so brown that he really shouldn't have been there any more. His friend on the other hand was still totally pale. Just as I was battling with the momentous decision as to whether or not I should smile sweetly over at them or not, suddenly the brown one waved jovially in my direction. This, of course, came as quite a surprise, but naturally I gleefully waved back and within two shakes of a pedigree siamese cat's tail they came shimmying over!

«It's really full here isn't it?» the pale one said. «What are you gonna do tonight?»

«Well, go to bed I expect!» I replied, and looked at the brown one.

«All on your own?» he asked. Now what was that supposed

to mean? Was he trying to set me up with the pale one? Or were they thinking of a threesome?

«I think I could really do with a good night's sleep,» I said, as I really had no idea what was goin' on. What were they up to and who wanted what?

And then, as we got chatting the pale one suddenly asked me, «What star sign are you by the way?»

That was the last thing I wanted, all that ridiculous star sign claptrap. I was just considering saying that actually I'm a kangaroo with wallaby in ascendance when Brenda came shooting up to me rescue.

«You know what, I'm really tired, why don't we take a quick look into *Metropol* and then head for home?»

«But really only a quick look,» I said to her, and then to the other two: «It was nice chatting to you. I'm sure we'll see you at the beach tomorrow, won't we?»

«Where will you be then?» the pale number asked.

«Somewhere in the first five rows,» answered Brenda.

I quickly gave the cute one a fiery look and then said goodbye to the Swedish girlies. Then we shot over to *Metropol*.

It really is only a couple of steps away, so being a thrifty gal I naturally took my half-full glass with me. But hardly had we battled our way through the madding crowds at the entrance when an overenthusiastic waitress dashed up to me and cried: «Please go back outside! That's a *Mykonos* glass!»

I mean really! How prissy can a girl get? Naturally I was so shocked that I threw my arms up into the air and as chance would have it the offending glass slipped outta my grasp. Then she started running around like a madwoman on acid coz she 'ad to sweep up the glass. But I must say that left me completely cold. Well, really! If they insist on building their club right next door to *Mykonos* they must surely expect the occasional queen to troll in with a glass from next door, mustn't they?

Anyway, the music in *Metropol* really was fab. They were

just playing the extended version of *Crucified*, and then came *Ritmo della Notte* which I just simply adore. And it was so full that a girl could hardly breathe.

«Well, I think we'd better save this for tomorrow, don't you?» I said to Brenda and so we set off home. I fell straight into bed without even taking my face off and went out like a light.

«Elvira, get up! Come and water the palms!» I heard Brenda calling after a while from somewhere miles away.

«What is it? It's still dark,» I groaned, still half asleep.

«Well open your eyes, and it'll be light then won't it!»

And so it was all of a sudden. The sun was shining like mad and the sky was so blue like it only very occasionally is at home in summer. So I sprang right up outta bed, though a slightly more subtle wake-up would've been nice, but then that's just the way she is, darling Brenda.

After me mornin' ablutions Brenda told me where the *Ansoco* supermarket was. It's the cheapest place in town for food shopping.

«Yes, and bring drinking water, too,» she said.

«Why? Is the well in the supermarket?»

«What well?»

«The one where I should get the water from!»

«Oh that one! Yeah, it's right next to the deli counter. But you'd better be careful you don't fall in!» she laughed.

So off I trotted, past *Nestor* and over the third planta in *Yumbo* where I then found *Ansoco* straight away.

There wasn't a well next to the deli counter though. There were just thousands of plastic bottles standing around with the word 'agua' on 'em. That's what everyone was taking. That's when I realised I would have been quite out of place in my special water-fetching drag!

When I finally got back home with the jam, butter, rolls, bog roll, water and all the other household essentials, darling Brenda had already laid the table and made tea.

«Oh, I really don't know what beach ensemble I should wear,» she complained. «What are you gonna wear then?»

«I'm wearing me light blue sun top with the wide neckline and pretty buttons.»

«What about a skirt?»

«Oh, I think something with a summery naval feel don't you? Me blue an' white striped shorts I think. What about you?»

«D'ya think I should wear the green and yellow cycling shorts?»

«They're a bit bold don't ya think?»

«Well, what else should I wear? I haven't got anything else.»

«You've got that pretty T-shirt with the block stripes and stitching. Why don't ya wear that? And those frayed bermuda jean shorts. That's always perfect for the beach, ain't it?»

So that's what she wore. Straight after breakfast we packed our dinky little beach bags and set off for the Atlantic.

To get there we had to traipse down the whole length of the Avenida de Tirajana till we got to an enormous hotel called *Riu Palace*. There we shimmied through a high archway and came out onto a massive terrace.

«Oh Gawd! It's the Sahara Desert, dear!» I said. I was totally amazed. Suddenly, all I could see was sand. As far as the eye could see, nothing but sand dunes!

«These are those world-famous dunes you usually only see on postcards sent from Playa,» Brenda very patiently explained to me.

At the end of the dunes you could see the sea just sitting there sparkling fabulously in the sun.

After I'd finally seen enough of this wonderful view I wanted to continue on to the sea. We couldn't though because the terrace was completely surrounded by an iron fence.

«So what now?» I asked, somewhat perplexed.

Brenda had already taken off her shoes and shirt and said: «Well, you'll just have to climb through the fence won't you?»

On closer examination I saw that one of the iron bars had been sawn out of the fence and people were crawling through the hole.

So that's what I did too. Well, that's not entirely true. The little gap was just somehow too cute so I decided to climb over the fence, just like you have to climb onto a boy's bike. That's when I noticed that most queens can't climb over a fence in the normal way! Brenda couldn't either.

«It's just not me, dear!» she said after she'd just squeezed herself through the gap in the fence.

«It's a bit like throwing a ball. Most queens can't do that either,» I said.

«Funny that. It's the same with whistling. Now, the lollipop lady, that's a girlfriend of mine, she's completely forgotten how to whistle. When she was still a naff she could whistle away like a good'un. And then after she came out she just couldn't do it any more. All she got was this quiet hiss! That really shocked her, I can tell you.»

It's really odd ain't it? I can't really throw properly either. Anyway, I was just about to set off, straight across the dunes to the sea. A normal person would always take the shortest route, wouldn't they?

«For heaven's sake,» cried Brenda, «that'll take you hours to get to the sea!»

«Why?» I said, «the sea is only just over there behind them dunes.»

«It just looks like that, believe me. The lollipop lady wandered around over there for two weeks the year before last and never found the sea. There are thousands of valleys between the dunes. You'd 'ave to keep goin' down one and up t'other and before long you'd come over all squiffy.» Now I really couldn't imagine that because it all looked so near but I trusted my best girlfriend, who is pure goodness through and through, and off we set diagonally to the right into the dunes. After a while we came to an area where there were a whole lot of crippled-loo-king trees and bushes and thorny rushes standing about. And we waded right through the middle, sometimes going off to the right, sometimes to the left, then straight ahead again and then diagonally. Between all this undergrowth there were always people lying around in the sand sunning themselves. At first it didn't seem all that odd; I just wondered what they were all doing lying around here, so far away from the water?

After a while we really did come to the Atlantic Ocean. It was at least two miles away from our house.

I added up just how far a girl could end up trolling in four weeks. Two there and two back, that's four miles already and if you do that every day for four weeks it's over 100 miles. But that doesn't matter on holiday, and a bit of exercise is good for the old tootsies anyway.

As I stood there at the ocean shore and looked out to sea I could really understand what Shirley Maclaine was on about. She really loved the sea and the salt, and I really loved her too.

«First of all we have to decide where we want to plant our-selves,» said Brenda. «On the sand or on a sun lounger?»

«Well, I'd prefer to have a sun lounger. I'm sure it's much more comfortable,» I said.

«I think so too. Especially as it's so windy today. We'd look like lady mud wrestlers if we got all nicely oiled up and then covered in sand.»

So we went on the sun loungers. They were all stood toge-ther in pairs with a big umbrella in between called a sombril-la in Spanish. I learnt that from this Spanish bloke who came shooting over to get his 900 pesetas for the two sun loungers and the umbrella. That wasn't exactly cheap. And there wasn't a shower either. But then again the sea and the sun were free. And of course, as I noticed straight away, this section of the beach was completely gay. There were some really gorgeous numbers lying around, and somehow everything was really relaxed and friendly. With quite a bit of squealing and furtive looking this way and that of course! After I'd been in the water and really enjoyed the waves, the holiday really started for me. The sun was shining fabulously, the sea was roaring, and no naffs as far as the eye could see! Now I could do with this at least once a year!

As I really didn't want to get totally burnt to a cinder I larded on the suntan lotion from head to toe. Then I realised that, even though it was a nude beach some of the guys still had their swimming cozzies on.

«Well, they're just shy,» said Brenda, and looked up from her Jackie Collins.

«D'ya think so, really?»

«Well, what else can it be?» she said.

«I think they just like havin' white arses!»

«Well let 'em then.»

«Ya know, I don't think that looks bad at all. In porn films they always 'ave white arses, don't they?»

«So? You thinking of the Hollywood career now, are ya.»

«Oh no, it's a bit late for that. I just think it looks good.»

«It doesn't look bad I s'pose.» Quite undecided, Brenda put down her book. «Should I put me cozzie back on then?»

«We'll 'ave to decide now. Otherwise it'll be too late.»

«Whata ya gonna do then? D'ya wanna stay white?»

«I'd like to. But I always go swimming in the nude and then I'm bound to forget to put me cozzie back on.»

«Why don't you just leave yourself a note on the sun lounger with 'Elvira, put your cozzie back on!'»

«Don't be daft. That's far too much of a palaver.»

«Well, I'm puttin' me cozzie back on. A white arse just looks better than brown all over.» And in a flash she had it back on.

On the other hand though, I really didn't think a brown arse is so ugly as to have to go through all that fuss with the ridiculous note!

Now I don't know about you, but when I'm on a nude beach I just can't help having a good old vada at other people's dangly bits, just to see what they look like. Sometimes you really do see the oddest things. But what really struck me this time was that most people had their pubic hair very short this year. Really short and well groomed. I must admit that was something I'd never considered until then.

But this pubic hair care thing really is a good idea. I mean, you don't just let the hair on your head grow totally wild, do you? You get it cut and shaped to set your head off to its best advantage, don't you? Now I'm not suggesting we should all rush off to Vidal's for a wash, cut and blow job, I mean blow dry, who would be able to afford that every couple of weeks? But a bit more care certainly seems like a good idea.

Anyway, I decided then and there to get the scissors out that very evening and thin out me riah down below and give it a nice shapely cut.

Just as I'd plugged in my Walkman, was having a good earwig of *Army of Lovers* and was nicely browning away with my eyes closed, all of a sudden something pinched my toe.

With a screech I leapt up and there was the pale bloke from *Marlene's* from the day before standing in front of me. His name was Jeffrey, and he was wearing beige bermuda shorts with kind of Egyptian hieroglyphics on them. On top he had an eau-de-nil *Lacoste* T-shirt on and the whole ensemble was set off by a charm around his neck with wings that also looked typically Egyptian.

«Well,» he said, «that's very nice of you to keep the sun lounger next to you free for me. Lovely weather isn't it?»

And all of a sudden he'd made himself completely at home and spread out a white sheet over the sun lounger, set up a dinky little head rest, and then spread a towel over the lot. Now the fact that the sun lounger next to mine was free really was a complete coincidence.

«Are you all on your own then today?» was of course my first question.

«Yes, Peter's got things to do,» he replied, and then he didn't say any more at all but just pulled this enormous book out of his bag and started reading it.

It was something about ancient Egypt. Yes, and then after a while he started rabbiting on about star signs again and just didn't stop.

«Yes,» he said,» before my present life I'd already lived twice. Once in ancient Egypt and once in ancient Rome.»

«How d'ya know that?» I asked, completely astounded.

«Well, my druid told me, of course.»

Then of course I had to ask the stupid question: «What's a druid?»

«Haven't you read *The Mists of Avalon* by Marion Zimmer-Bradley?» he asked, quite accusingly. «A druid is a Celtic priest.»

«Didn't the Celts die out ages ago?»

«Of course. But their secret knowledge survived, and that's why there are druids again today. I just had a weekend seminar with my druid last September. It was fab and only cost £ 200.»

«And why d'ya do it?»

«I need it for my spiritual well-being. For finding myself in the widest possible sense. Otherwise we are all just drifting in soulless nothingness, neither Yin nor Yang, somewhere in between, do you understand?»

«Yes,» I said. Of course I didn't have a clue what she was on about! «And what did the druid actually do then?»

«Well, first of all we all stood around outside like the stones at Stonehenge. Then the druid calculated the precise cosmic energies and then we started with the planet dances. I was Saturn. That's the planet with the rings. We really danced ourselves free. I could feel space, the whole cosmos. It was simply fabulous,» he enthused, still totally high on it. «And then we

34

cleansed ourselves. With sage steam and fans made from eagles' feathers.»

Well, I really couldn't picture this Jessy as a planet! She probably just danced the hoola hoop and got dizzy! And then she claims to have been Saturn. I was going to say «What about Uranus?» but thought better of it. In any case he warbled on for ages about metaphysical energies, energetic heaps and waking powers till my head began to spin.

«Yes, an' how did this druid discover you 'ad already lived as an Egyptian?»

«He simply possesses the power to see people's previous lives. He just can. You can't explain everything with logic. I know now that I was a doctor at the court of the Pharaoh Akhenaten.»

Have you ever noticed that these reincarnation queens were always in top-notch positions? I've never heard anyone say, «I used to clean Nefertiti's toilet.»

«I can remember so much,» she went on. «Particularly Akhenaten's death as I had a really bad time after it.»

Then I had this sinking feeling that he'd tell me all about the move, as in the novel *Sinuhe the Egyptian*, which I particularly enjoyed reading, where it's described in great depth.

And then off she went. «You know, after Akhenaten died the whole court moved out of the capital Akhetaten and back to Thebes. I'm telling you, it was frightful. The heat, the masses, and me with my entire household on this clapped-out old Nile boat. I still shiver at the thought of it today. Thank Amun that a crocodile didn't pull me off the skiff and eat me alive.»

He probably wore naff *Lacoste* shirts back then too, I thought. The sight of them probably frightened the crocodiles straight back into the water.

«And Tiye,» he went on, «the new pharaoh's wife, she was a miserable old goat. You can't imagine how I suffered under her. She wanted to have me killed.»

«No, really?» I gasped. But in reality the whole story didn't interest me in the slightest. I don't know what I would have done in Tiye's shoes. This Jessy was a total pain in the arse even in her third life. I'd probably've shoved her in the Nile too.

«Tell me,» I suddenly thought, «how did you actually die? Did somebody kill you or did you die a natural death?»

«Well, you know I really can't remember,» he said. «Somehow I must just have woken up one morning and I was dead.» Now that was totally baffling to me, how someone like this Jessy could forget her own death.

«Yes, now I can remember my death in my second life really well. They burnt me in the Roman Forum. But what happened in Egypt? I've thought about that for months, but it just simply won't come back up.»

«But they mummified even their cats and crocodiles in ancient Egypt. Why shouldn't they have mummified you then?» I asked him.

«Yes, of course they would've mummified me and buried me somewhere in the desert,» he replied. «But since the eleventh century BC the ancient Egyptian grave robbers have defiled all the graves. And probably mine too. And then in the Middle Ages the Christians considered mummy dust to be a powerful aphrodisiac. So the Arabs dug up half the desert and made massive profits out of the Christians' potency crisis. Who knows what happened to me then.»

«It all sounds very complicated to me,» I said, and put some more cream on me nose. But then he pulled a big old reference book out of his bag and started leafing through it and then let out a big sigh.

«Do you think that could be me?» he asked after a while, and shoved the book under my nose.

Naturally I took a good look at the photo. *Middle dynasty. Mummy. Not identified* stood underneath it.

«Well,» I said. «I can't tell. Why don't you ask your druid?»

«Mmm,» he said then. «I'll definitely do that later on.»

«How come?» I asked flabbergasted, «is he here on the island?»

«Yes, you've seen him. I was with him at *Marlene's* and in *Mykonos* yesterday.»

God, did that give me a shock. That brown number was his druid. Then I had to go and leap into the water to cool off and stop myself from having a screaming fit.

When I came back after quite a long time, Mystic Meg had thrown herself at Brenda. And I heard Brenda asking her: «What does all this reincarnation stuff actually mean to you?»

«Well,» replied the Jessy. «Somehow it just makes me feel really good. Somehow totally secure in the unending flow of history.»

«Mmmmm,» was all Brenda replied.

Somehow there must be something like providence. I mean, who could have guessed such a thing? There you sit, minding your own business in *Café Marlene*, and all of a sudden you're lumbered with a druid!

I always consider it to be our duty to overcome stupidity and avoid nonsense. But that druid did look gooood! And if he'd have wanted me, maybe he'd have made an old Egyptian witch doctor outta me too. Or I'd have spent the rest of the holiday sitting at the Atlantic coast as a reincarnated Egyptian charlady! These druid queens can be quite fierce you know.

### WHAT IS THE REAL TROPICAL SECRET OF VELVET-SMOOTH SKIN?
### OR: HOW TO GET BROWN IN A FLASH WITHOUT SEEING RED!

I can't be doing with this bloody suntan lotion business all the time! Continually discovering the tropical secret of velvet-smooth skin. I can't stand it! But if you don't do it within two shakes you look like a shrivelled old prune, so you've got no choice. And there's no end to it. Somehow you're always rubbing it in. Brenda always says, «Better well greased up than always screamin' Aaaarrrgh!» But that's not much consolation.

First thing after I get up in the morning I rub some of that pre-sun stuff in me face. This is supposed to last till we get to the beach. Then I usually go for a swim and lie in the sun for about an hour without anything on to speed it up a bit. But then it's high time for the main event, so I lard that on all over. And then after about an hour or so, once I've been in the water again and most of it's gone, I have to go through the whole process again. And so on and so on, at least three times a day! Then when I get home I wash off the remains of the sun cream and rub on the after-sun lotion. Honestly, somebody really should invent something to make the tropical secret just a little bit easier.

And then all that jargon with the protection factors. I've never understood that either.

«Well,» says Brenda, «if you use factor 4 you can lie in the sun four times as long without getting burnt.»

Well what's that supposed to mean? Suppose then I lie in the sun for an hour without getting sunburn? And if I notice it's coming on I whack on the 4 cream. Then it takes a total of 5 hours until I get burnt. No, somehow they must have got that one wrong!

And then there's this ridiculous factor 12. That must be for anaemic sleepwalkers or something. If I get to the beach at ten thirty in the morning and lie in the sun for an hour without any protection and then cover myself with factor 12 then I'd have to lie around until nearly midnight. Whoever in their right mind would do such a thing? Usually the beach is almost empty by half past four anyway coz it's so cold and windy.

Anyway, I could've sat around on the beach 24 hours a day if it hadn't got so cold and dark every time. No one day was like another. Every day we had new experiences.

«What d'ya think then?» somebody who was sitting in the sun with his friend on the next sun lounger suddenly asked me. They were what I call bone dry numbers, if you know what I mean. I generally refer to them as BBC: brown, boring and constipated.

«What, eh, about what?» I replied, somewhat surprised.

«You and your companion seem very normal. Don't you think we should sit in the first row tomorrow?»

«What for? It's quite nice here in the third row isn't it?»

«Haven't you noticed how much harm that does us?»

«What?»

«The way those people there in the first row are behaving. That rubs off on all of us. Just have a look.»

Of course I had a good look straight away and was naturally very surprised to think I may have missed something. But what I saw didn't exactly knock me for six. Sissy was lying there with her girls. She's a good honest East End girl. And next to them were some leather ladies. Once there were five of them on one sun lounger having a good kiss'n' cuddle and they did let out the occasional shriek. But apart from that there was really nothing going on.

«You have to consider that they are lying in the first row. All the normal people go right by them. Families with their children. You know? That's bad for us.»

39

«How come? For us?»

«I presume you are homophile too?»

I just nodded, though maybe I should've said, ‹No, I'm an X-File me›, well, I've always fancied David Duchovny!

«Yes, well, can't you see how they are behaving? The way they look. Two of them are wearing rings around their genitals. One of them has pins through his nipples. And look at the shoes that one is wearing.»

I must admit I hadn't noticed her with the shoes. She had on these big butch black lace-up boots with thick woollen socks sticking out the tops. Apart from them all she had on was a cock ring, golden tit-clamps and extremely short hair. Well, those boots in that heat on the beach really were a bit out of the ordinary.

«Oh heavens above,» Brenda suddenly chipped in. «What on earth are we going to do?»

«I already suggested to your companion that we should sit in the front row tomorrow.»

«Well!» gasped Brenda, and clasped her imaginary pearls in mock horror.

«Normal people must be really shocked by that sort of thing,» the old BBC-lady whined on. «If we all lie down in the first row then no one would even notice that this is a homophile beach.»

«D'ya think the normal people would like that?» I asked, and did the double pearl clasp, for emphasis.

The other BBC-lady just raised her eyebrows and said, «Well, of course they would.»

«Elvira, what do you think? Should we sacrifice ourselves for the naffs?» Now Brenda never calls me Elvira in public, maybe Theresa every now and again, but never Elvira. So of course I knew exactly what she was up to.

«Well Lizzy, if you come with me and we tell Molly and Trixie and Daisy and they could bring along Pussy Galore and

Curly Shirley from Purley then I'm sure we could fill the front row.»

«Right,» said Brenda, «You let 'em know and I'll get me knittin'. It'll be fab. The naffs won't notice a thing!»

Naturally the two BBC-ladies didn't say another word! I mean really, where would we end up, making ourselves invisible? After all, naffs run around however they want to. But you wouldn't believe it, the next day the BBC-ladies really were in the front row. Now I thought that was very brave, stuck in the middle of all that screaming. Just like a kind of safe harbour in a hetero storm.

Now personally I'm with Gloria Gaynor on this one. «I am what I am.» And isn't she right? You can't just be like the naffs want you to be. You have to know who and what you are. And if you fancy men then you fancy men. And that's all there is to it. Once I knew this engine driver from Birmingham. She'd never heard of Gloria Gaynor either. «No,» she'd always say, «I can't stick all that screeching, it always gives me such a start.» Well, I always jump a mile when a puffer-train lets off its whistle right behind me. So there you are, people really are just different!

But this *chauffeuse de train* was always a bit down in the dumps. She'd come all the way to Playa without her boyfriend.

«Why didn't ya bring 'im along?» I asked her.

«He wants to wait until the summer before goin' on holiday.»

«Where does he wanna go then?»

«To Bulgaria, to the Golden Coast.»

«Is that still so fashionable for you Brummies then?»

«No, but he's still into revenge-tourism at the moment.»

«What on earth is that?»

«Well, for years we used to go on holiday behind the Iron Curtain, and nearly starved to death many a time.»

«How come?»

«Well, as they had no idea about the free market and earning money and complicated capitalist things like that, if they didn't feel like serving you they just didn't. We often went into completely empty restaurants where all the staff were sitting in the corner playing cards or something, and if we tried to get served they'd tell us all the tables were reserved for some coach party they were expecting any minute. One night when we hadn't had a bite to eat all day, he threw a fit and ran through the streets screaming, «Food! We're starving! Food!» at the top of his voice. So now the tables have turned he likes to go back and, well, you know, get his revenge!»

Of course things are very different today, but even in Playa a girl could easily starve to death. So just to be on the safe side I always took an apple and an orange along with me. And if I needed a pee I'd just pop into the sea. Everybody did that though of course not a soul would admit it. That's what they were all like in Playa, «The truth is a virtue, but I'm not telling it to you!» Then again, the things they'd come out with when they were overdue for a good despunking!

«I think I'll just go for a little walk,» Brenda'd always say and then shoot off and just leave me there alone on the beach for hours on end. But usually she'd just sneak off while I was having a quick forty winks.

And Heidi, she was from the Swiss Alps, she would always say: «I'm just going to look for shells.» But of course she never came back with any shells. There aren't any on the beach at Playa.

«Where are they all running off to?» I asked Vera.

«Into the dunes. For a bit of bongo-bongo!»

Somehow I'd thought as much. So naturally I had to go and explore for myself. Just to see what was going on, of course.

Now this Bongoland sort of starts gradually. You have to go inland from the beach into the dunes where the trees and bushes are. First of all I kept to the left. Sort of towards the lighthouse. You see I'd noticed the occasional figure trolling around in that direction. As I got closer I could see this was the rush-bongo area. All the girls were trolling around between these enormous rushes that were as tall as Lily in her stillies. There were lots of narrow walkways and cosy little resting-places where you could set yourself down and let yourself go. Well, I must say, my most successful outings were with the rush-bongos!

Later, when I told Brenda about this she said, «Well, that's no surprise. The rush-bongos'll take anything that's still wandering about at three o'clock.» She can be sooooo wicked! But queens didn't invent wickedness; they just perfected it to an art form!

So that you don't get lost in Bongoland you really need to draw a map or at the very least take a compass with you. Once I got completely lost and had absolutely no idea where I was. So I climbed up onto the top of a kind of hill to see where I was. It was really quite comfy up there. As well as the fabulous view there were lots of little sandy hollows where you could lie down and have a rest. But, as I soon found out, most of these seemed to be inhabited. You see, this was where the hill-bongos made their nests. When a hill-bongo was in a good mood he'd climb up onto the top of the hill and wave his tackle. Then you could see from a long way off that he was waiting for a visitor. This courtship ritual would go on for varying lengths of time. Some would wave around for hours without any reaction from the others. On the other hand, if another bongo showed some interest, sometimes the first bongo would stop waving and just walk away. That meant: «Go away! You're not what I'm after.»

If, on the other hand, both bongos liked each other they would usually stand in silence for a while and wave at each other and then jump down into the hollow and do bongo-bongo. As I continued on my way I saw that in the areas in between, the ordinary sand-bongos had their settlements.

Compared to the hill-bongos though, this variety of bongo

was much more sociable. They can usually be seen in whole colonies and are always chatting and squawking. And sometimes they can be quite wicked too.

As I passed one of the colonies I heard one of them say: «Look at her! She must've had a Caesarean,» referring to me! Just coz I've got a big appendix scar!

Where the undergrowth is densest is the capital of Bongoland, so to speak. I really can't describe it any more exactly. But any half-respectable queen with a bit of international experience will have no problem finding it!

You can tell you're in the capital coz of the traffic on the highways and byways. Traffic lights would come in quite handy. But on the other hand I had the impression things seemed to be flowing quite freely and everything was regulated in a kind of biologically dynamic fashion!

Yes, and just as I was promenading along on one of these cosmopolitan boulevards, minding my own business, I suddenly heard a voice.

«Hello, Miss Totterheels. Good afternoon. Welcome to the elephants' graveyard.»

It was the anthropologist Dr. Fappy-Hanny calling out to me. She works in the bowels of the British Museum.

«What are you doing here?» I asked, somewhat surprised to run into a respectable lady like her on such wild terrain.

«Well, you see I'm doing a study on the social behaviour of the bongos.»

«And you have been learning their customs, I see.»

«Oh no, no!» she denied vehemently, and went on to explain how she got her scientific material.

«And you, Miss Totterheels, what are you doing here?»

«Oh, I'm just collecting those delicious Canarian mushrooms that ...»

«Now that is an interesting pastime,» she interrupted me. «I didn't even know that mushrooms grow here.»

«Oh, haven't you heard of them, Dr. Fappy-Hanny? Apparently it rained last week, so they should be shooting up all over the place.»

As this line of conversation was obviously going nowhere fast, I decided to simply change the subject.

«Dr. Fappy-Hanny, do you know why the capital city of Bongoland is actually called the elephants' graveyard?» I asked.

«No, I'm afraid I don't. I just heard it from some Dutch friends of mine last year and sort of adopted it.»

«Okay,» I said, «I'll adopt it too then.»

Somehow it was very fitting though. All the undergrowth was very grey and dead-looking. Maybe the bushes couldn't take all the sperm that people had deposited on them. Protein poisoning or something like that. Maybe the vegetation just couldn't swallow it, as one shouldn't nowadays anyway! Obviously this phenomenon would have to be investigated by some ecology expert to say for sure. Maybe David Attenborough could do one of those fascinating nature programmes on it on BBC 2.

Oh, and I just remembered, all of Bongoland is actually a nature reserve. So it's a total disgrace the way some people leave all their coke cans and beer bottles and newspapers and placky bags and all that sort of stuff lying around. But that's just by the by. In any case, there's plenty going on. As Vera would say, it's nose to nipple down there! But you couldn't keep your nose on someone's nipples for too long because you couldn't resist looking around. Even the Pope couldn't troll through Bongoland without having a good old shufty at the goings-on.

Now, the colonies of the common sand-bongos usually lie close to each other in the bushes. Whenever you come across these groups it's a bit like wandering into a stranger's front room without ringing the bell. Usually a well brought-up girl would ring the bell and say, «coooey!» The sand-bongos don't expect this though. They're much more adapted to the through traffic of the roaming-bongos.

As I was wandering through the undergrowth of the ele-phants' graveyard I wondered: Have the sand-bongos settled here because they know the roaming-bongos come by or do the roaming-bongos go by because they know the sand-bongos are here?

When I posed this fascinating philosophical dilemma to Vera later on she said, «The question of the sand-bongos and the roaming-bongos is like the chicken and the egg. Not a soul knows which was there first!»

On the other hand, Gerty reckoned that the sand-bongos are just too lazy to walk and so they just wait till the roaming-bongos come by. Now I've come to believe the sand-bongos lie there because they know that the roaming-bongos come by and the roaming-bongos just like to wander. It's a kind of natural division of labour. Both are just dependent on the other. It's what they call a symbiotic relationship. It's not that I'm an ex-pert or anything. We learnt about things like this in biology at school. It's like those crabs wot live in the shells of them snails.

So this is how the sand and roaming-bongos are dependent on each other. It usually begins like this: when a roaming-bon-go passes a colony of sand-bongos, then all the sand-bongos look up and stretch their necks. How they do it, however, de-pends entirely on the genus (that's yer actual Latin for type) of roaming-bongo that comes past. With some specimens they only look very briefly, with others a bit longer. But it never co-mes to pass that a sand-bongo doesn't look at all. This indicated quite clearly to me how well adapted to each other they are.

If a sand-bongo takes a fancy to a passing roaming-bongo it jumps up and runs after it. Then both of them troll about a bit around the elephants' graveyard, and after they've gone through the willy-waving ritual the sand-bongo usually lures the roaming-bongo into its lair. There they get down to the ac-tual business of bongo-bongo.

But not always. Sometimes they just run back and forth for

hours on end. That's why the streets of Bongoland's capital seem so lively. These bongos just can't make up their minds. They usually think: maybe there'll be something better-looking just around the next corner. And then they spend all day wandering around and end up totally pissed off coz they didn't get anything at all. The bongos will never admit this though. They always say, «I really wasn't in the mood. I was only checking it out!»

After I had made a small protein donation to a needy German sand-bongo from Cologne, I wandered away from the elephants' graveyard towards that hotel, the *Riu Palace*, which seems to loom over the goings-on like some kind of majestic white castle.

Gradually the area became less densely populated and I began to concentrate my attention more on the beautiful landscape. And then, all of a sudden, as I quite innocently came around a bend minding my own business, I bumped right into a female! I was shocked! Now who would expect such a thing in Bongoland? She was just lying there stark naked on her back in the sand with her legs spread as wide as the Dartford tunnel, and was grinning at me invitingly!

Naturally I made a hasty getaway. And then, just as I was recovering from this rather disconcerting encounter, I saw this naff and a naffess squatting in sandy hollow. At least I thought they had to be naffs.

But then as I carefully looked more closely the naff suddenly began waving his equipment just like a regular sand-bongo! I don't believe it, I thought. Bongos always nest alone or in colonies, but never with a female!

The naffess, that is to say the naff's female companion, just sat there looking and smiling. And then she whistled after me! And the pretend-bongo just kept on waving and waving.

Now I was totally confused. I felt completely bongoed out. And as I was just contemplating how incredibly varied the world can be and what manner of weird things an innocent girl can stumble across, I remembered this book by Goldilocks Ellis I once read. Now, she reckons there are pure bongos and pure naffs and all sorts of bits and pieces in between. It must've been one of those I'd just run into. Or maybe it was a kind of transitional-bongo. In any case, Goldilocks would've shrieked with joy if she'd seen that mixed-up number back there in the sand. And doubtless she'd've whipped her slide rule out and started taking her weird measurements again.

I just ignored the bongoloid number and continued on my way and was quite relieved when, after a while, I came across a perfectly normal colony of sand-bongos. I felt much more at home, and then I bumped into Heidi again.

«Don't yoo vont to go home soon? Brenda's already vriggling around impaishuntly on her sun lounger.»

So I hurried myself up a bit and stopped inspecting the goings-on quite so closely. And Heidi came along with me back to the beach. «Vot are you ladies up to tonight?» she asked me.

«Oh, nothing really,» I replied, «the usual.»

«Zat is not good all ze time. I 'ave to 'ave a bit of ze culture evrry now and again I doo.»

«What're you doin' then?»

«Vell, I'm going to ze *Bavarian Cellar* in *Cita*. Dunja Rajter's giving a guest appearance zere tonight.»

«Oh yes, I heard about that on the radio.»

«Don't yoo vont to come along too zen?»

«Well, I'm not sure ...»

«I zink Dunja is totally fabulous, and so brrrave. She comes here to Playa and zings her heart out. Alzo her sister just got completely bombed out in Yugoslavia.»

«Really, bombed out?»

«Yes, it vos terrible. And she still zings all zem zongs.»

«Even that one about Alexandra? *The horses so gay, the wagons so ragged*?»

«Yoo mean *Gypsy Boy*?»

«Is that what it's called?»

«Yes, but it's ze ovver vay round.»

«What d'ya mean, the other way round?»

«Well, *ze wagons so gay, ze horses so ragged.*»

All that bongoing must've got me quite mixed up to go and forget a thing like that. When we got back to the beach Brenda was sitting there all packed up and ready for take-off. «Where 'ave you been all this time? Everyone thinks you've turned into some kind of sexmaniac. And the first bell for *Marlene* has already gone.»

«So? We usually don't leave till the second bell anyway.»

«Well, I'm cold. Let's go now anyway. I'm dying for something to drink.»

Now, these bells for *Marlene*, you can't actually hear them. You can only see them. We noticed in the first week that the girls always set off from the beach in three waves. When the first cool breeze came along in the late afternoon, that was the first bell. That's when all the chilblains gathered up their things and scooted off to *Marlene's*. About half an hour later the cool breezes started coming in a bit more often. And that was the second bell. Then they started setting off in droves. And then another half-hour later when it got even cooler, you saw the third bell setting off. After that the beach was pretty empty. Only the really weather-beaten ones could stick it out then. Vera, she's one of them. She'd hang around on the beach until you really couldn't stand it any more. Unless of course you happened to have a gas stove with you or you collected sticks in Bongoland and made yourself a nice cosy little camp fire.

Now I must admit, I do tend to feel the cold a bit. Brenda doesn't. That's why we'd always head off on the second gong. After that you can't get a seat in *Marlene's* anyway.

At any rate, just as we'd set off and were making our way through Bongoland this totally hysterical naffess came running

49

up to us. She was wearing nothing but a frilly pink towel and a most pained expression.

«I've been robbed! All my clothes are gone! I can't go back to my hotel completely naked.»

«Oh heavens above!» cried Brenda. «Have you still got an apple Elvira? Then at least the poor woman could do the Adam and Eve routine while running hysterically through the streets of Playa.»

Of course I'd already eaten my apple. But then two very charitable sisters came up with a blouse and a skirt for her and off she shot, happy as a sand-bongo.

Now, if you want to be alone in Bongoland, and you choose to leave your clothes all alone while you go off to enjoy yourself, you naturally have to reckon with the worst. And as a queen you can't exactly run naked into the hotel with nothing but an apple and a smile either. You'd at least have to have the op first or nobody would fall for that routine!

It reminded me of the time Brenda phoned me up in the middle of the night from Sitges where she'd gone off on her own for an adventure hol. Close Encounters of the Mediterranean Kind, as she was wont to say. She was totally hysterical and I couldn't understand a word she was screaming. I finally got the gist that she'd been robbed and lost her wallet, money, credit cards, the lot.

«How on earth did it happen?» I asked her.

«Well,» she replied, «I went into this darkroom and took all me clothes off ...» I mean honestly. What do you expect?

All in all, that was a very odd day.

When we finally got to *Marlene's* we sat around for at least half an hour without getting served. None of the serving wenches took any notice of us. They just stood around in front of the mirror fiddling with their hair and squawking in Spanish.»

«Do I need this, after the day I've had?» I said to Brenda.

«Ooh I know, dear!» she said, and then suddenly I saw the

Queen Bee and Alessandro passing by. I know the Queen Bee from Manchester and Alessandro's her other half, but he usually lives in Venice.

Now, the Queen Bee is rather rotund and has the habit of wearing tight, horizontally striped T-shirts. Very fitting as I'm sure you can imagine. That's why Alessandro christened her the Queen Bee. But Brenda always calls her 'Buzzing Bertha'. She thinks that suits her better! Anyway, they were just passing so of course I called out, «Coooey!»

«Why are you sitting here? The cakes and the coffee are atrocious here,» said the Queen Bee. «Why don't you come with us to *Café Wien*, the food's much better there.»

Seeing as we were having a good old moan about the gaff, that seemed like a good idea.

But just as we were about to set off Brenda suddenly started calling out «Coooey». She'd just spotted Bob and Rob, a delightful Brummy pair that always spent Chrimbo at Playa. They were totally inseparable. What Bob wouldn't do for Rob and what Rob wouldn't rob for Bob was nobody's business!

«Come with us to *Café Wien*,» Brenda suggested.

«Yes, maybe,» said one of the Brummies. «We have to wait for Jacques and Pierre from Nice though, they're very nice!»

«Oh, there they are now,» squealed the other one, and then ensued a ridiculously long greeting with lots of *enchantés* and *bonjours* and *fantastiques* and so on.

The Queen Bee, who'd been waiting for us, started flapping her wings impatiently and cried, «Well, what's going on Elvira? Are you coming or not?»

«Yes, what's going on Bob?»

«Are you coming or aren't you?»

«Just wait a minute. I'll just ask Pierre if they want to come too.»

«Oui,» said Pierre, «j'adore le gâteau autrichien.»

«Non,» said Jacques, «Aye 'av to go to se toilet.»

«There's a cottage at *Café Wien* too, ya know,» said one of the Brummies.

«Well, I don't know about you but I'm going,» said the Queen Bee.

«Save us a seat,» Rob called after her.

«Regarde, là bas,» said one of the Frenchies suddenly to the other.

«Over there,» chimed in Rob.

«Mais non, Peter, Paul et Mary viennent ici.»

«Yeees!»

«Merveilleux.»

And off they all went gabbling at once.

«The next thing Mary Poppins'll come floating down on 'er brolly,» I said to Bob.

«Now don't start bitching, Elvira!»

«I'm not bitching at all!»

«I need a coffee,» said Brenda, and just ran off.

«What's up with Brenda?»

«Oh, she just wants 'er coffee.»

«But we want to go to *Café Wien* too. Why doesn't she just wait for us?»

«Maybe she had to powder 'er nose.»

«Hey Rob, how many pesetas have we got left?»

«Why?»

«Peter, Paul and Mary haven't changed any money up yet. Can we lend them some?»

«I'll just have a look. Oh my god, Bob! Where's my wallet? My wallet's gone!»

«Look for it properly first.»

«I have.»

«Oh, sorry. I've got the wallet.»

«Heavens, did that give me a shock.»

«Avez-vous assez d'argent pour nous aussi?»

«He's just counting it.»

«All these Spanish coins. I can't tell 'em apart. You count it Robbie.»

«We've got about 2000 pesetas left.»

«That's not enough. I'll just go and change some with Pauline. Wait for us will you?»

«Oui!» everybody said.

«Really! Enough is enough!» I thought, and went over into *Café Wien*.

It's only a few steps behind *Marlene's*, and when I got there the Queen Bee, Brenda and Alessandro were sitting there, now accompanied by a couple of Brussels sprouts. I had no idea who they were! In any case they were chattering away to each other in French. And when they spoke to Brenda it was pretty ropey pidgin English. And then in came Vera and Luigi. Of course he babbled away with Alessandro in Italian and with Vera in Brummy. And when Alessandro spoke to the Queen Bee it was back to English. And then, you wouldn't believe it, in minced a couple of Polish girls. They lived in Switzerland, and as well as German they spoke pretty good French so they got on well with the Brussels sprouts. I tell you, Babel had nothing on us! It was like the Eurovision Song Contest without the singing!

But the apple tart with cream and the eggnogg tart really were fabulous. And the coffee wasn't the murky ditchwater they served up at *Marlene's* but proper Austrian mocca, delicious. After that we nearly always went to *Café Wien* after the beach. In actual fact it was a completely straight café. But when we all rolled in from the beach *en-masse* it was almost completely de-naffed for about an hour.

And while we were all sitting there, suddenly one of the girls said, «Why don't we all go out to eat together tonight?»

And then they all started again.

«Let's go to *Bistro*.»

«Oh not again. We were there the day before yesterday.»

«Well then, what about *El Chaco*? That's in *La Sandia* too.»

«Oh, not on your nelly! It's so dark in there.»

«But the food is really good there.»

«I'd like to go to *El Chef*. It's nice there.»

«But that's so far away.»

«No it isn't! It's only about a hundred yards from *Yumbo*.»

«Yes, but not in the centre. More like right at the edge.»

«I think we should go to *Casa Vieja*.»

«What? To San Fernando?»

«We'd have to get a cab then.»

«Yeah, but it doesn't cost much.»

«Don't forget *Casa Vieja* is always so full.»

«Oh, when we were there it wasn't too bad. Just a bit loud, that's all.»

«Then why don't we go to *Pomodore* and have an Italian?»

«I hate pizza. I'd rather just make meself a sarnie!»

«Then have something else.»

«You know, I quite fancy a nice paella.»

«Oh no. Those paellas are silly.»

«Then let's go to *Bistro*.»

«Oh no, not again ...»

And all of that in Polish, English, French, Italian and Brummy! I thought I was gonna have a fit. But then we somehow managed to settle on *Bistro*. Now we just had to sort out what time to meet up!

«Why don't we meet at nine in front of *La Sandia*?»

«But everybody goes at nine. I really can't stand the crowds you know.»

«Well eight then.»

«Are you mad? I'll never be ready in time.»

«Can't you hurry yourself up a bit?»

«I am on holiday, you know!»

«Why don't we go at ten?»

«Oh don't be ridiculous! If we go at ten we'll still be eating at midnight.»

«Well let's say eight thirty then.»

«I don't know if I'll manage that.»

«And what about nine thirty?»

«Oh, but I'm meeting somebody at eleven.»

In the end we went to *Bistro* at nine. It took nearly an hour until we'd agreed on time and place. But anyhow, at a quarter past nine we were all standing outside *Centro La Sandia* and could finally go and eat. After all that I was completely exhausted.

«Going out to eat with nine queens is worse than ... well, I really can't think of a comparison,» I said to Brenda afterwards.

«The only thing worse is going out to eat with ten queens!» she said, and you know, she's quite right! On the whole, Brenda and I didn't actually go out to eat much at all. Brenda's a wiz with the cooking and I'm a wiz with the washing up so that's what we did. On Christmas Day we flung a bit o' tinsel on the palm trees in the garden, watched Her Maj's speech on BBC World, and had a delicious six-course dinner with two bottles of fabulous red wine. It really was very cosy. And then we put the telly on again and watched the Spanish King do his speech. Of course we didn't understand a word, but we noticed straight away he wasn't wearing a crown! They've got no idea, these Continental Royals, 'ave they?

«You know,» I said to Brenda, «it's quite a nice change having a King on the telly at Chrimbo. You really can 'ave too much of Queens sometimes.»

«Ummm!» was all she had to say to that.

And so we chatted for a while about Kings and Queens and such, left out *Nestor's*, and headed straight for Mykonos at half past twelve.

Well, it was so full there that a girl could easily have had an attack of claustrophobia. The whole balcony from *Tubos* to *Metropol* was packed like a tin of sardines, as if the world and his wife had arranged to meet there. I was really quite concerned that this thin balcony might just snap off and we'd all end up cascading down in a cloud of dust into the Norwegian pub!

Actually, from about the 20th onwards the whole island seemed to just fill up more and more. All the time we kept running into old friends. Luckily we weren't continuously being confronted with the same old irritating tinned Christmas tunes on every street corner like you get at home. They just don't have that in Playa. Now most of the bars were pumping out Jingle Bells half the time, but usually in that catchy pop version by Boney M. And that we could just about bear.

I only actually heard Bing dreaming of a White Christmas once, and I mean, who would dream of such a silly thing anyway? After all, we hadn't come to Playa for sledging, had we?

Once we finally got into *Mykonos* it took us ages to find the Brummies. We'd arranged to meet them there, you see. But making arrangements like that is actually a complete waste of time in Playa. You can't help bumping into each other all the time. Rob was quite beside himself and could hardly keep still. I couldn't help wondering if he was havin' a White Christmas after all, or if he'd just had too much sugary dessert again!

«Well,» she said, «I've been here for three whole days now and still haven't fallen in love.»

«But you've got your Bobbie.»

«I've got him all year. I know I'm on 'oliday, but a change is as good as a rest!»

Bobbie was obviously also taking time out from the marriage. At least, we could see him busily flirting around in a corner of *Mykonos*. Every now and again he'd shoot over to let us know how far he'd got with one or other victim. «Well, Bernd is really very nice. He comes from Cologne and is staying in those pretty *Sonnenland* bungalows. He's already invited me to spend the night.» But after two hours they were still there.

«Well, that Bernie really is a dizzy queen. First he's flirting with me like there's no tomorrow, and then all of a sudden he sees someone else and off he goes leaving me all on me own. Now I'm all charged up, what on earth am I gonna to do?»

«Why don't ya go for an emergency shag in the darkroom?» suggested Brenda.

«But it's so full in there, you need to order tickets days in advance. I might as well take a look in though.»

Bobbie was hardly gone and Roberta got on her high horse. «You'd never catch me going into the darkroom. It really lowers your market value quite substantially!»

When Bobbie finally came out she seemed quite relieved and certainly in a much more agreeable mood. I think darkrooms really aren't such a bad idea for an emergency shag. But as Bobbie came out of the darkroom I noticed that his trousers somehow looked funny.

«Hey Bobbie, what's up with your skirt? It's flapping around a bit innit?»

«What? Have I burst a seam?»

«No, but something's not quite right.»

As Bobbie grasped her thighs she suddenly let out a piercing shriek. «Oh Heavens! Where's me belt? Me belt's gone.»

«It can't be.»

«Oh my God, and on Christmas Day of all days. I had it before, I know I did.»

«Well, you really must've been goin' at it not to notice someone pinchin' ya belt.»

«I didn't notice a thing, honest.»

It really was gone too.

Now all the thieving that goes on in them darkrooms, that really is a nasty business. You really wouldn't believe what the girls pinch off each other. But most queens don't like to talk about it. They're ashamed coz then they'd have to admit to having been in there in the first place.

«A lady simply doesn't do such things,» they always say. But as the night draws on, the fewer ladies there are around.

It's the same all over the place. And some of them just stand around for hours as if they're waiting for James Dean to come back from the dead or something.

Now Robbie was quite different. She got straight to it. But first of all she had to do the whole lovey-dovey thing. Otherwise it just wouldn't work for her. This is a typical woman's problem. But I can well understand it. I mean, you can't just fling yourself around somebody's neck. At least you have to start it off slowly.

«Look Elvira, doesn't he look cute?» That's how Robbie would always begin.

But what awful taste she had! Quite impossible. Usually it was German trade that she always fell for. They generally looked like you might imagine Mimi in *La Bohème*. She died of whooping cough or something like that as well, didn't she. Anyway, Robbie always went for types like that. As thin as possible, and sort of undernourished-looking. Of course they didn't have to have a cough. But they did have to have a 'tache. Otherwise something was missing.

«Don't you think he's cute, Elvira?»

«Well, he's not really my type,» I said then.

«He's got such really open eyes!»

Well, what can you say to that? As if all the others were standing around in *Mykonos* with their eyes closed or what?

«Yes,» I said, evading the point. «And he's kind of looking around with them isn't he ...»

«Yes, so dreamily and yet so open.»

«Exactly.»

And then she'd carry on like this for a while praising him to high heaven, and then shoot off. On Christmas Day she'd also grabbed herself a German coughing Mimi and was in her element. And once again I was left standing around like an unwanted side dish at the Banquet of Love.

But as a consolation prize I had a lovely chat with two very nice numbers. They'd got dressed up all Christmassy. One of them had very short hair and was wearing a kind of smock made out of lacy kitchen curtains with the inscription *The Early Bird Catches the Worm* crocheted on the back. Under that he had on a top made of black stiff-looking fly mesh which was held together at the shoulders by wide white zips and flowed straight down to the waist where it was tied like a Cossack's skirt with simple parcel string. Under that he had tight red trousers, also made of fly mesh, and to round it all off heavy black stillies with chrome buckles of the type you might wear to stamp out a forest fire.

The other one was featuring similar footwear, though her legs were bare up to the knees where they disappeared into kind of knickerbocker-like linen underwear with a frilly trim. A moss-green brocade sofa cushion with deer and forest motifs served as a sleeveless top. A mini leather jacket, tarted up with gold spray paint, hovered just above her hips and stylishly rounded off this camp Christmas ensemble.

Well, next to those two in my denim skirt and simple raspberry blouse I felt almost plain! But we had a lovely chat about fashion and questions of style. And after that I went straight off to bed. And I for one certainly slept peacefully.

But Christmas certainly isn't as peaceful as people always say. Some people have the most terrible tiffs at Christmas too. For example, the next day Brenda and I went down to the beach and Henriette and her friend Eddie were sitting in stern silence, flatly refusing to speak to each other. They were from Milton Keynes, and were always to be found in the front row too.

«What's up with you then?» I asked Eddie.

«Well, Henry treated me most brutally yesterday.»

«On Christmas Day, well I never!»

«He obviously doesn't love me any more.»

«What did he do then?»

«Ravioli!»

«Ravioli? For Christmas dinner? That's barbaric!» Brenda almost fell off her sun lounger.

«It's mental torture! You can get a divorce for things like that.» Eddie was still fuming.

«How did it happen?» I asked.

«Well, we actually wanted to go out for a really nice meal. But for hours Henry just kept saying 'yes yes' and then all of a sudden it was eleven o'clock and he just opened a tin of ravioli and said Merry Christmas.»

Well, you can't put up with that sort of behaviour now, can you? Apparently Eddie just ran out of the house and cried her heart out. Now if Brenda'd done that sort of thing to me I'd've given her a good slapping. It took right up to the next day for the two of them to make up. It was a terrible day.

Although it had all started off so fabulously. Not a cloudette in the sky, fantabulosa beach weather and enchanting waves. Brenda lay around on her sun lounger chatting to the Brummies, Vera and Gerty discussed the religious aspects of running a household, and the *chauffeuse de train* did press-ups and kept clapping her hands in between. Everything was quite peaceful and the sun shone like mad.

I was quite innocently letting the waves wash over me when all of a sudden I saw someone with outstretched arms lying in the water on her stomach letting the waves carry her up and down.

Now, everyone knows that queens come up with the most bizarre ideas of how to have fun on their hols. On Christmas Eve one of them swam around with an advent wreath on her head, and a few days earlier some Swedes performed scenes from the Nativity in the waves. Well, on her hols a girl can do just whatever she wants, that's what I always say. And that's why I said to myself: let her play at being drowned if that's what she enjoys.

After a couple of minutes I vadared over again.

Well, hat off to 'er, she must have lungs the size of the bags under Barbara Cartland's eyes, was all I thought. Then suddenly an enormous wave washed over me and just as I was getting back up onto my feet I noticed she was still just bobbing about like a rubber duck in a three-year-old's bathtub. She's really good at that. It looks very convincing, I was just thinking. But at the same moment the thought struck me, maybe it wasn't a show after all.

And off I went like a torpedo in a Speedo! Now the water really wasn't that deep, just about came up to the chest. It was just the waves that kept crashing over my head.

When I finally got hold of her and tried to turn her over onto her back she kept slipping outta my grasp like a lychee at the Chinese coz she was so greased up.

And she didn't react at all. Me, at Christmas, on a mercy mission with a drowning man in the Atlantic! «Help! Help! Help!» I shouted as loud as I could.

Hardly twenty metres away a whole throng of queens was frolicking in the waves. When at last they heard me they just stared with gormless expressions on their faces. They probably thought we were practising a traditional Canarian Christmas water ballet or something. At any rate, they only stared and grinned.

When I didn't stop screaming and had managed to heave the unfortunate chap into somewhat shallower water so that I could hold his head at least a bit above the water, a couple of the bathing belles came paddling over. The three of us then tried to manoeuvre the unfortunate gentleman onto the beach.

Now let me tell you. Don't think for a minute that this kind of thing is easy. This person was so well oiled up that you couldn't get a hold on him anywhere. And he was heavy an' all.

Then all of a sudden a particularly high wave splashed right over our heads. The shock of it made us all let go of him again.

And in no time he disappeared in the spray, so that for the next minute or so we had to dive around like demented ducks until we found him again.

I'm telling you it was really frightful. But after a while we actually managed to get this poor person onto dry land. His eyes were completely turned up in his head and a strange white bubbly foam was coming out of his mouth. Of course someone immediately tried to resuscitate him.

And as I knew that this Irish doctor always lay around in the fifth row of the sun loungers, I flitted right over to fetch her. But she must've been off exploring in Bongoland. So helplessly I trotted back down to the beach.

By this time thousands of people were standing round gawping and I heard someone say: «He's been dead for hours!»

Now I'm certainly no expert on drowned tourists. But somehow I had a feeling she was right. Anyway, all our heroic efforts at Baywatch were a total waste of time.

In the meantime the Spaniards that reign sovereign over the sun loungers had called up the Red Cross on their walkie-talkie thingy. And sure enough they came steaming down the beach with all the trimmings.

«Well, that was 'is last oil change,» said Brenda as they shoved him into the ambulance and carted him off with flashing blue lights and sirens.

Now, how on earth the chap could drown at all was a complete mystery to me. Maybe the unfortunate soul had a heart attack or something. Or maybe he just lost consciousness or hit an iceberg much further out and was slowly washed ashore. How on earth were we to know? At any rate, I was totally exhausted. I collapsed onto my sun lounger and didn't want to see or hear a thing. Life can be soooo cruel. One minute you're larking about in the sun and the next thing you know you're stiff as a board, bloated out with half the Atlantic in your lungs and some geezer in a white coat is shoving you in the fridge at the morgue. I can certainly think of more pleasant ways to cool off after a hot day on the beach!

Of course it soon got around that I was the one who pulled the poor chap outta the water. When we got to *Nestor's* a few hours later people kept looking over, putting their heads together and giggling like four-year-olds. And when we arrived at *Mykonos* later on, I myself heard some spiteful queen exclaim to another: «Oh look, here comes Pamela Anderson!»

They've got no respect for the dead, these girls. But then, that's just the way they are!

## Sun, Fun and Nights of Delight
### Or: I bet Karen Carpenter came to Playa once too

Now I don't know what it's like for you with men, but I nearly always have the same problem: the ones I want don't want me and the ones that want me I don't want! It's enough to drive a girl completely mad.

«Ya don't really want 'em, that's your trouble,» Brenda always says. «You're deliberately avoidin' 'em.»

«I'm not trying to avoid anyone. I just want something stable,» I said.

Of course Brenda just rolled her eyes and drummed against her temples with all her fingers like some kinda demented sea anemone. She just doesn't understand me.

And then, shortly after Christmas, we were sitting on the terrace sipping our Campari and oranges when all of a sudden the phone rang. «Who on earth can that be?» I asked.

«The man of your dreams, no doubt.»

So off I shot to the phone.

«Hello, this is Philippe, I'm a friend of Jack's. Would it be all right if I popped round to use your washing machine?»

Now, Jack was a friend of mine from Bradford.

«Of course,» I said. «When do you want to come round?»

«Straight away if that's OK?»

«Oh all right,» I said, and hung up. «D'ya know someone called Philippe?» I asked Brenda.

«Yeah, he's a friend of Jack's. I didn't know he was in Playa too.»

Philippe came trolling round with his washing about an hour later, and as I opened the garden gate I knew straight away: this is the one!

Do you know that old classic «*I'm on the Top of the World*» by the Carpenters? Well, that's just how I felt when I set eyes on Philippe. Just like Karen when she was singing her heart out, bless her.

And after we'd stuffed Philippe's washing in the machine and were planted back on the terrace with our Campari and oranges I soon realised that Philippe didn't only look fabulous but he was really nice too. I was totally besotted.

«I certainly won't be avoiding this one,» I thought, and beamed amorously at Philippe. And he kept on beaming straight back at me.

As I heard the machine was already spinning, I thought I'd better think of something pretty quick.

«Brendan and I were thinking of going to the *Eden* tonight. Why don't ya come along?» I asked.

«I'd love too. Let's say nine thirty.»

My knees instantly turned to jelly.

«You're not hangin' about today are ya?» cackled Brenda as soon as I'd seen Philippe to the gate. «I didn't know we were going to the *Eden* tonight.» But we were there at nine thirty, and so was Philippe.

And it was really fab. With every half-hour that passed it became clearer and clearer: it was him or no one at all.

And then, at midnight, Philippe suddenly said: «I have to go now or Jim'll lock me out.»

Oh no, just my bloody luck! I thought. He doesn't already have a boyfriend does he?!

Brenda just couldn't help giggling all the way home.

But the next evening we were sitting on the terrace when the phone rang again.

«Now who can that be?»

«It's bound to be Philippe with 'is dirty knickers again.»

So off I shot.

«Yes, this is Jim. Can I come round and use your washing machine too?»

Hardly half an hour had passed and there he was sitting on our terrace. But he obviously had a special reason for making this his washing day. Even before the washing was done I knew full well I could forget all about Philippe. He was well and truly accounted for. This Jimmy had him firmly in his grasp.

So you see, that's the way it always goes. You've hardly set your sights on a man and all of a sudden you're a widow. I was so depressed that the first thing I had to do was knock back some eggnogg. With some coffee powder on top. It's always good for widows' hot flushes. And then I put on my *Carpenters* tape. At least that's something you can rely on throughout all life's ups and downs. «*I'll Say Goodbye to Love ...*» Oh, she was so right. I wonder if Karen Carpenter ever spent her hols in Playa. She probably rented a bungalow with her brother!

Anyway, then we often went to the *Eden*. Not just coz Philippe was always there but because the music was fab too. Show tunes! The kind of stuff that holds heart and soul together. Somehow terribly simple and yet moving.

For example, that one about the majestic liner with its most precious cargo, bringing my loved one from New York to Glasgow! That helped salve my Philippe wounds a bit. And he always stood right beside me and smiled so sweetly. I really had to pull myself together to stay strong and not completely crack up.

What really got to me was the Shallala song. It fitted so exactly to how I felt about Philippe, and went like this:

> *Shallala, I need you. Shallali, I love you.*
> *You will never cry, that I promise you,*
> *For you belong to me and I belong to you.*
> *And if you're all alone and your heart is feeling blue,*
> *Then just remember that I am always there for you.*
> *And as the years go by and you get old and grey,*
> *I will say to you, just as I do today.*
> *Shallala, I need you. Shallali, I love you.*

Now there are times when that kinda thing's just what a girl wants to hear, rather than that ear-shattering disco stuff all the time. Especially when she's having troubles of the heart.

But maybe one day Philippe will read these lines. Then he'll know that even today I like to think of him.

> *I think of you and the wild butterflyyyy*
> *Maria Angela – good byyyye*

That was one of them songs too. They played it the evening that I saw Philippe for the last time. Now that bit with Maria Angela of course doesn't fit one bit. You'd have to make a special jessy version out of it first.

But I never met a Mario Angelo! Just that Luigi from Palermo. Him and Vera and Gerty and that very manly OAP's nurse from Wolverhampton, Dave, they were often in the *Eden* too. Except for one night. Then they weren't speaking. At first I didn't even realise what was going on. Then I noticed it smelt funny.

«Oh God, what's that awful stink?» I asked quite innocently and had a good sniff around Vera. But she smelt quite normal. And after I'd got a good whiff of Luigi and Gerty and got to Dave I couldn't help coughing.

«Did ya get into a fight with a skunk, or what?»

«This *eau* is probably all the rage among the Welsh,» jibed Gerty.

«Oh, you don't even know where Wolverhampton is, you.» And so it went on.

«Oh come on girls, let's go to *Mykonos*. It should be hotting up just about now,» I said. «I'm sure we can all relax there.»

But little did I know it was only just getting started. Dave and Luigi started doing that wrap-your-legs-around-each-other dance. You know, it's a kind of dirty dancing thing where you thrust your leg between the other person's and rub up against them really close, almost falling over till either one of you creams your panties or the record ends. And that in the middle of the crowd. Luigi with his fabulous body, his skin-tight cycling shorts and his muscle vest was making such a scene that all the girls were gawping.

Gerty of course was not at all amused, but Vera just kept laughing all the time. When the record was over and Luigi was making his way out of the menagerie this elderly Scottish lady rushed up to him and groped him front and back as if she was about to try and toss the caber. Luigi was obviously not familiar with this national sport and clearly didn't fancy the idea of being tossed on the dancefloor of *Mykonos*.

By the look on his face you wouldn't've been surprised if there'd suddenly been thunder and lightning. Obviously sensing that his Sicilian masculine pride had been wounded, his hot Mediterranean blood came straight to the boil. In a flourish of passionate Italian screams, he simply smacked her one. Well, the poor old dear practically fainted and just stood there, nailed to the spot screaming «Help, I'm being attacked!» In Scottish of course. Then suddenly the music came to a halt and everyone just stopped and stared, wondering what on earth was going on.

Well, the waitress came shooting straight over to try and negotiate a peace settlement. In Spanish of course. And then finally Gerty had to add her two pennies' worth to this multicultural fiasco an' all. Now why she had to get involved remains a mystery to me, but she really let rip into Dave and Luigi like a madwoman. In English of course.

«Look Elvira, isn't it nice to see European Unity in action?» said Brenda to me as Gerty shot by us with a face as red as a beetroot without saying a word. And right behind her came Dave and Luigi. Vera just stood around looking very embarrassed for a while and then left too. The next day, on the beach, the Gang of Four was together again. But none of them was speaking to one another.

«What's going on here?» I asked.

«They've all got it in for me!» said Gerty.

«Yes, Gerty was extremely rude to us.»

«What did she say then?»

«I'm not saying, but it was outrageous!»

With that they all gazed heavenwards with indignant expressions.

«Well, what did she call you? Dozy tarts?»

«Worse!»

«What? Silly bitches?»

«Worse than that!»

«Ooh! I know! Old whores?»

«Much worse!»

«Well, what did she say then?»

«She called us cheap sluts!»

«No I did not! I said you were behaving like cheap sluts.»

«It's not the 'sluts' bit that I object to. But 'cheap', that's just going too far.»

«It's not going too far at all.»

«You're just frustrated coz you didn't get off with anyone, that's all.»

«I didn't want anyone.»

«Oh what? You mean no one wanted you coz you're so bitchy.»

«I'm not bitchy!»

It's always the same. When the girls can't think of anything else to say in their arguments then it's because you didn't get off with anyone. And that's supposed to explain all the complicated things that are going on in a really sensitive person!

«Always wanting to knob everything that crosses yer path. I just don't think it's right, that's all,» said Gerty. «A quickie can't always put the world to rights you know.»

Oh, she don't tell no lies!

Now do you remember Freddie the blacksmith? She often got quite frustrated too.

Now usually when queens get frustrated they bitch at each other and mercilessly spit poison all over the place. Frederica was quite different though, a genuine exception. He just hammered naffs. Then he felt much better! And when this blacksmith went a hammerin', things generally stayed nailed!

I was so glad I met him. Some time between Christmas and New Year we had arranged to meet in *King's*. At three o'clock in the morning!

Actually I generally didn't like *King's* very much coz it didn't get going till so dreadfully late. And also because I was quite afraid of walking round that side of the *Yumbo* so late.

«Don't be daft!» said Freddie. «You just go straight along the main road. Then at some point you come to the chemist's, and I'll be waiting for you on there.»

«Make sure you're on time!» I said, and set off from home at a quarter to three. And at three sure enough I saw Freddie standing outside the chemist's.

As we were walking down the deserted street, a skinny little Spanish queen was trotting along a way in front of us. I bet she's going to *King's* as well, bless her, I was just thinking when all of a sudden two fat, stuffed, pig-ugly and obviously completely drunk naffs appeared out of nowhere. They started chasing after the little Spanish queen shouting something in Scandinavian.

«I know them,» Freddie said. «They're Norwegians. They're staying in my hotel.»

«Is that supposed to make me feel better?» I said. Now in situations like this I always have a kinda sixth sense. And it was saying to me: something's gonna happen!

Now good old Quentin Crisp always used to say in situations like this you should just hold your head up high and walk briskly away from the pack. A gentleman should walk but never run. And I do believe that was what the little Spanish queen tried to do. But the fat pigs soon caught up with her and one of them grabbed her by the blouse.

«Oh Gawd! What should we do?» I thought, and had a good look around to see if there were any more girls nearby that we could round up. But there weren't.

Now I don't know how it happened, but all of a sudden one of the fat Norwegian naffs was lying on the ground, with the little Spanish queen underneath him.

Next to me, Freddie started snorting like a steam train going up a hill.

«Leave this to me. I'll sort 'em out!» he bellowed. And then it all happened in a flash.

Like a bat outta hell, the hoof hammerer shot off towards the mugger. First he landed him a hefty kick up the arse and then yanked him off the squashed queenette. No sooner was she free than she ran off into the night. Then the other naff jumped onto Freddie's back, grabbed him round the neck, and tried to get him in an armlock. He didn't manage it though, and Freddie got hold of his wrist, bent over, and whisked him very skilfully over his shoulder onto the ground. At the same time there was a horrible crunching, cracking sound and the Viking oaf suddenly looked up with a very pained expression. He grabbed hold of his wrist and screamed something in Norwegian that in English probably meant about the same as «Aaarrghh!» Anyway, he was a bit preoccupied for the time being.

But then the other naff, who in the meantime had got back on his feet, suddenly whacked Freddie one over the head, and then again. And then it really kicked off – a right regular butch blokes' punch-up!

Up until this point I'd had no idea just what a butch number I'd arranged to spend the evening with! Well really! This hoof hammerer went at it like Ivan the Terrible. I really couldn't bear to watch. In less time than it would take your average lamb to even think about shaking its tail twice he'd polished off the second naff an' all. This one started wailing in gibberish and spurting blood out of his nose. To add insult to injury, more queens turned up and began ogling the spectacle, so they decided they'd had enough and staggered off.

Now to be perfectly honest I must say I'm more of a born again Florence Nightingale than a born again Ivan the Terrible myself. In any case, in spite of all the excitement, I just had to make sure Freddie wasn't hurt. But he wouldn't let me anywhere near him.

«Aaaaaargh, I'm so angry! I'm so aaaaaangry!» he kept shouting, and snorted like an orangutan on heat. And then he couldn't resist screaming «Stupid arseholes!» after the two defeated Vikings.

«Let me 'ave a look. Are you quite sure you're not hurt?» I said.

«Ah, leave it out. This ain't the first time I've knocked some sense into a couple of apes!»

And all he had was a few grazed knuckles on his right hand. Apart from that there was no sign of any damage at all.

When we'd finally got into *King's* and had a few stiff ones to calm us down, purely for medicinal purposes needless to say, I suddenly remembered that Freddie had said the two naffs were in the same hotel as him.

«Yes,» he said. «They're two or three floors above me.»

«Why don't you move in with us? At least just as long as they're still there? We've got enough room in our house.»

«Just let 'em try it. I'll knock their blocks right off for 'em!» he said, still in quite a rage. And that's when I realised there are gay men too who actually like a fight. It just goes to show. You live and learn, even a wise and weary old queen like me!

But guess what? That wasn't the end of the story by any means. The next day we squatted most impatiently on the beach waiting for Freddie to turn up to see if anything more had come of it. And it had. Quite a lot in fact.

You see, one of the naffs had to go to hospital. Compound fracture of the wrist. So then the other one phoned his family back home in Norway to let 'em know what'd happened.

Three or four days later Freddie came down to the beach with more news. «That guy's brother arrived from Oslo yesterday evening. Now him and his friend keep followin' me about. I really 'ave to keep a lookout.»

«Are you quite sure you don't wanna move in with us?» I offered again.

«Naw, if they start I'll really give 'em a good seein' to. I'm just waitin' for the word.»

«Heavens above,» exclaimed Brenda. «It's practically a war.»

«But we didn't start it. It was them naffs. If they behave themselves then Freddie won't do anything to 'em, will you Freddie?» I said, with a look on my face that was a cross between dressage rider and boarding school headmistress.

«Well Freddie, just don't let 'em provoke ya, that's all,» Brenda added thoughtfully.

«But that's just exactly what they do. They start imitatin' drag queens whenever they see me. If they do that just one more time I'll knock 'em to kingdom come, I'm tellin' ya.»

After that we didn't see nor hear a thing from Freddie for two days. We were starting to get really worried. But then he turned up again and looked quite normal.

«Yes,» he said. «The brother that came over from Norway, he's in hospital too now.»

«What??!»

«No, really??!»

«Yeah, fractured skull.»

«For heaven's sake! How did that happen?»

«Him and two other blokes kept takin' the piss outta me. If you don't pack that in, you're gonna get a good hidin', I told 'em. I s'pose they didn't believe me. Anyway it all kicked off again.»

73

«And who started it, you or them?» we asked, still quite sho-cked.

«Them of course. Right in the middle of the hotel lobby. They suddenly went for me and so I just grabbed an ashtray and whacked 'im over the 'ead wiv it. It was self-defence. The police let me go the next day too.»

«What?! You were in prison?»

«Yeah. They called the pigs and an ambulance straight away. They carted the brother off to hospital and threw me in the nick.»

Well, we were quite at a loss for words. My inner nurse star-ted having palpitations again.

«But Freddie, you can't just go and wipe out the whole fa-mily!»

«Exactly,» chipped in Brenda. «We queers would die out too if there weren't any more naff families!»

«I didn't want to, but they really started it. The rep at the ho-tel was my witness. She told the cops that too, that's why they had to let me out the next day.»

«Where's it all gonna end? They haven't got any more anti-gay sons in that family by any chance, have they?» asked Vera.

«It doesn't look like it. You see the father's s'posed to be fly-ing into Playa today.»

«Let's hope he isn't bringing the entire Norwegian army with 'im for revenge,» said Brenda.

«Naw, I don't think so,» said the hoof hammerer. «The rep said she's spoken to him on the phone and explained what's been goin' on. Apparently he's quite reasonable. He just wants to speak to me.»

«Uh-oh, that could mean trouble,» I thought. The two gol-den boys of the family both smashed up and hospitalised by a queen, now that must be pretty tough for any father to deal with, I'd've thought. But then we all have our cross to bear!

At any rate, I bet that little Spanish queen never had the slightest idea what would've come of her trolling off to *King's* that night. I kept a look-out for her in the bars and on the beach, but I never spotted her.

«Yoo could zpend veeks looking for herr and not find herr,» explained Heidi to me. «Zese Canarian tomato pickers all look ze same. Zey'rre all small wiz black hairr and brrown eyes.»

«Oh I dunno, you can't say that,» I replied. «There are a few that look quite different.»

«Zen zey must be blind!»

«What d'ya mean by that?»

«Vell have a look at zat vun over zere,» said Heidi, and pointed to a little Spanish thing flitting around on the beach. She was obviously trotting around after this very butch-looking tall, blond, north European number.

«I mean, just going on looks alone, Mickey Mouse and Ronald Reagan would've gone together better,» Brenda pointed out.

Now I must admit I'd first noticed this strange pair a few days before. The little Spaniard always trotted along about three steps behind her husband, with her head bent forwards as if she were in disgrace. He held her hand and strutted forth purposefully as if marching off to war and at such a speed that she regularly got dragged along behind him. I couldn't help wondering if this was where the expression «drag queen» had originated from! Whether they were runnin' through the dunes or off to the water, it was always the same sight.

«She haz to be blind!» exclaimed Heidi.

«Oh what. She's probably just never heard of women's lib» said Brenda.

«Now come on girls. We're not in the Middle East ya know.» I said.

«Vell it certainly izzn't normal, ze vay she let's 'erself get drragged about like zat.» This was Heidi's considered opinion.

«She isn't blind,» said Vera. «The two of 'em are always here at this time of year, they're madly in love. They've been chargin' about like that for five years now.»

«D'ya know 'em then?»

«Sure. The guide dog chappy always says he's from Iceland. But when he's had a few too many he forgets and talks with a thick Scottish accent. He's a plumber from Glasgow. And the Spanish queen's from Bilbao, she trades in antiques. They met each other years ago here on the beach.»

«Oh my Gott, vot a palaver!» exclaimed Heidi. «I couldn't stand zat. Zere's probably about a sousand miles betveen zem.»

«Well they can't exactly yodel to each other from one mountain to the next like you lot in Switzerland, can they?» Brenda's always so practical, bless 'er heart.

«Apparently it gives the little Spanish queen a sense of security being dragged around the place like that all the time. Each to their own, dear. You just have to accept that!»

«I know, it doesn't bother me. It just looks so odd, that's all.»

«What do you mean odd?» suddenly Gerty was getting involved too. «That's genuine love that is.»

«Exactly!» said Vera. «Their holiday's over next Sunday. It'll be terrible. I bet they'll be in *Mykonos* sobbin' their little hearts out.»

«Oh how sweet,» said Brenda.

«Oh how orrful,» said Heidi. «Don't zey see each uvver for ze whole year zen?»

«Dunno. But there's always the phone isn't there?»

«Vot? A telephone relationship? Zat never vorks out,» Heidi knew. «I vunce had a lover frrom Milan. And Grotli and Milan are not as far frrom each uzzer as Bilbao and Glasgow. It drrove me into poverty I can tell yoo. I had to take out a loan to pay ze fone bill. And I took a zecond job too.»

«Cleanin'?»

«Yes! How did you know zat?»

«Oh I dunno, I just guessed.»

«Maybe they only call each other at night. That's a lot cheaper.»

«Tell me, where exactly is Grotty?»

«Grotli! It lies in ze canton of Uri.»

«Oh I know. I remember that from crosswords. Swiss canton with three letters.»

«Why doesn't the plumber just move to Bilbao? I mean they must have burst pipes and stuff in Spain too, don't they?»

«Uri sounds a bit funny tho' don't it? I mean sort of old fashioned, like dinosaurs or something.»

«You zink so?»

«Yes, don't ya think?»

«But dinosaurs haven't been around for ages now, 'ave they?»

«No they 'aven't, have they?»

«I mean the jock would 'ave to learn proper Spanish first of course. Otherwise it couldn't work.»

«Maybe she can already.»

«Of course nobody really knows why they all died out.»

«What? Has she got some kind of incurable disease then? But the healthcare system in Spain isn't too bad is it?»

«I read somewhere that they all got knocked out by meteorites or something.»

Now you would think a girl might run outta things to say when she's a lyin' and a bronzin' in the sun on the beach all day. But no, not at all. There was always something interesting to talk about. And from the sun loungers you could really keep a good eye on all the comings and goings. Especially if you were in the first few rows. It was just like having a season ticket to the National Theatre, the dramas you saw ...

However, Heidi would keep running off to Bongoland every now and then. She really had the hots for a Japanese chap she'd spotted. He was usually lying around in the dunes somewhere with his boyfriend. «Zis Ming vase really duz look vunderful,» she kept enthralling. «Huff you zeen hiz legs? Zey are full of muscles. I like zat.»

«Don't keep callin' 'im a Ming vase.»

«Vell, wot should I zay zen? Rice bowl?»

«How about Lotus Blossom, that sounds much nicer.»

«Or perhaps Daughter of the Rising Sun.»

One day as Brenda and I were heading through Bongoland on the way to the beach we saw Heidi's Ming vase almost have a heart attack. He was startled by one of those odd-looking little lizards that flit around in the undergrowth there, and leapt up with a shriek.

«Oh look,» said Brenda. «There's a Nip in the air!» She can be sooo wicked at times!

«Aw Gawdluvvaduck!» cried Gerty, and jumped up. «We'd better turn the Swedes over quick or they'll get burnt to a cinder.»

«Oh God, yes. I'd completely forgotten about them. They've been asleep for at least two and a half hours in the same position,» I suddenly realised.

«Wake up little Suzy! Wake up!» sang Gerty, and ran up and down the next row giving them all a good shake. «Wake up quick or you'll get completely burnt. And nothing ruins a Sunday dinner more than burnt Swedes!»

It's always the same with the Swedes. They always have to set off at two in the morning or some such ungodly hour to get through all that snow to the airport. So they never bother going to bed beforehand. Then, when they get into Playa in the morning they just dump their stuff in the hotel and shoot straight off to the beach. But of course they're so shagged out that they just fall straight asleep.

And when they wake up that's often the end of the holiday for 'em. They just stand around each night in *Mykonos* looking like the catch of the day at a lobster restaurant and moan about their awful sunburn.

«Now you'd think Queen Silvia'd give 'em each a dinky little travel alarm and sound instructions to get well and truly creamed up. They can't even do that properly,» said Gerty. But unfortunately they just don't listen to her in royal circles!

Now if you ever see any of these pale and interesting Nordic numbers asleep in the sun, give 'em a shove, shake 'em about a bit, and give 'em some sound advice: «Wake up! Don't get burnt!»

The Brummies, Rob and Bob, became particular specialists at this. They even offered a free oiling and creaming service. But only because they really had the hots for anything Scandinavian.

Just goes to show that very few people are genuinely selfless! This became very clear to me when suddenly we became the victims of a tidal wave.

I honestly don't know where it came from. But at any rate we did notice beforehand that there weren't any Spaniards on the sun loungers in the first three rows.

«Verre are all ze paellas?» asked Heidi.

«Strange, I can't see any either.»

«Maybe they've all gone into the water. The waves are really nice and high today,» said Brenda. And she was right, even though there was hardly any wind.

«Then they must have taken their clothes with 'em,» noticed Vera, and at that very moment there was a wild crash and an enormous wave washed right over us.

«It's ze end!» screamed Heidi, just as she and Brenda flew off their luxury loungers right in the middle of the breaking wave. I just about managed to hold on, but I felt as if I was going through the spin cycle in the washing machine.

«Bloody cheek! This isn't what I booked!» cried some queen from Surrey behind us, and all around the girls were shrieking and screaming as if the world was coming to an end.

Now it wasn't so bad. All our blouses and skirts got wet and full of sand, but they soon dried out again in the sun. What was much worse was that all the tubes and bottles of sun creams and lotions and all the stuff the girls kept under their loungers got washed all over the beach. It was as if a dam had burst and washed half of Boots all the way to Playa.

Luckily I found my *Tesco's* own dermatologically tested, eco-friendly, wide-band sun factor 12 lotion in a jiffy. After all, it got five stars in the Which Guide to Sun Preps. And also it was the only *Tesco's* bottle floating around amongst all them expensive ones.

What a lot of bickering that was! Especially about the Clarins and Lancaster tubes. Loads of queens had 'em. And they're not exactly cheap you know. And as you know it's not exactly the world's best-kept secret that lots of queens are pretty tight-fisted. In any case, it took at least an hour until peace could be restored.

But the wave did have its good side. For some this was the first time they'd come into contact with the water at all. They sat around on the beach for weeks but never actually went into the water.

For example Goldfinger. We called her that coz she always had half a ton of gold chains around her neck, arms, ankles and waist. In fact, that gold-rush fad had come and gone about twenty years ago, but she was clearly oblivious. And she never went into the water either. Just once it looked as if she was about to, but Brenda screamed out: «Aw Gawd! She can't go in the water.»

«Whyever not? D'ya think the waves'll rip off 'er riches?»

«It's not that. She'll go down like the Titanic with all that lot on.»

«Maybe she just wants to cool 'er jewels a bit. Ya know what it's like in the sauna. Chains can get awfully hot there too.»

And so it was. Goldfinger just tip-toed to the water's edge, bent down and scooped up a handful of the Atlantic, slapped it on her chains, and waddled back to 'er sun lounger and continued roasting.

Now I couldn't do that. Too much sun and I get hot flushes. At least once every hour I have to trot off and cool myself down.

But one afternoon when I came back from my hourly plunge there was a very strange atmosphere in our camp. It was totally quiet and not a soul was speaking. They were all squatting there as if they'd lost their voices. One of them was picking her toe nails, another was rearranging the contents of her beach bag, and most of the others were just staring absently into space as if there was something interesting to see.

«What's going on 'ere then? Have you all been bitchin' at each other again or what?» I enquired quite innocently. Nobody answered. Now these girls can be pretty moody, but this was most unusual. After a while though, as I let my gaze wander over the neighbouring sun loungers, I suddenly got a shock. Quite horrified, my eyes came to rest on the body of a bloke who was sitting on the next but one sun lounger to my left. «Oh God, Brenda,» I whispered. «What's up with *him*?»

Brenda didn't even look over. «I think that's really courageous of him to come an' sit 'ere,» she said as she brushed some sand off her lounger with the back of her hand.

«What is that? What's he got?» I really couldn't help staring at him. His whole body was covered with brown and purple blotches. All over – face, arms, legs, stomach, back totally covered.

«Kaposi's Sarcoma of course,» answered Brenda in a low voice.

Up till then I'd had no idea that it could look so bad. It really gave me quite a shock. And as I was sitting there practically in a trance I heard the two chaps next to me saying, «No, we don't smoke, sorry.»

Then I saw the bloke with Kaposi's with a cigarette in his

hand getting up and coming over. He was pretty big, well built, about late thirties.

«Have you got a light?» he asked with a nervous smile.

I nodded, picked up my pack of ciggies where I kept the lighter in, managed to fumble it out, flicked it on and held the flame up to him. But just as he bent down the wind blew it out.

«Let me do it,» he said. I handed him the lighter. It took a short while until the cigarette was alight.

«'Ave ya just got 'ere?» Brenda asked.

«I arrived a week ago,» he said, and then he told us he'd been coming to Gran Canaria on holiday in the winter for years. And so we struck up a conversation. First we just chatted about this and that, and once the ice was broken we also spoke about AIDS and the terrible situation.

«Of course I wondered whether I ought to come to the beach in my condition,» he said. «But I can't just sit around in the apartment all day. That's enough to drive you mad.»

«Are you in Playa on your own?»

«I always used to come with my partner, but he died six months ago and I just wanted to come back here. But I think it was a mistake.»

«Why?»

«Well, you know the gay scene just doesn't tolerate sickness. Everything has to be perfect, beautiful, and nice. And I'm not perfect anymore, not beautiful. And as for being nice, I can't even do that any more. And so you fall through the net. You're an outcast among outcasts.»

«But I think you've done the right thing coming to the beach,» I said.

«I think I'm like some kind of walking safer sex poster. But at least that's something I s'pose, isn't it?» and he managed a wry smile. «When I got infected people really didn't know that much about AIDS. At least today people know how to protect themselves.»

We chatted away for quite a while and then went into the sea together. But Michael, that was his name, didn't stay in long.

«I have to go,» he called over to us. «I'm meeting my brother and his girlfriend in Maspalomas at half past three. Are you gonna be here again tomorrow?»

«From about eleven,» Brenda called back.

«Enjoy yourselves,» he called and waved goodbye.

«He's quite right you know,» said someone suddenly in the water next to us. «People should just get used to the fact that AIDS affects all of us.»

We stayed in the water for a while. It was just too much fun, havin' a good splash about with all the girls in the sea. Mrs. Simon Smith from Battersea was always over the moon when a big wave came along. She looked like one of them dumb blondes in a game show on ITV that waddle around holding up cards with numbers on. Whenever a particularly large wave broke she would strike a ballerina pose right in the middle of the wash, with her back to it.

«Yes,» she said, «actually I always wanted to be a ballet dancer. But I never found anyone to catch me when I did those high jumps. So you see that's why it's so practical with these waves here.»

Except of course when there was a high wind blowing. That was anything but practical. That was when I had the most enormous trouble with my hair. I'd hardly got myself comfy on the sun lounger and got me riah set just nice when a big beastly blast of wind'd come along and blow it all over the place. Now of course for some people a strong summer wind blowing their locks all around can look most enticing. So carefree and natural somehow. But not for me!

«Your 'ead looks like a burst horsehair mattress,» Brenda said when she saw my hair standing up on end.

«I'm absolutely at my wits' end. This salt water. It's so hard on yer riah. Particularly when you've got such thick hair.»

83

«Then why don't you put a swimmin' cap on before you go in t' water.»

«Oh no, I know I'm camp, but I'm not that camp! Have you ever seen any of these queens 'ere goin' into the sea with a swimmin' cap on?» Brenda shook her head. «There you are then. Don't expect me to go setting fashion trends!»

But then I had a fabulous idea. Each day, shortly before we set off for the café, I made my hair completely wet and then combed it and sat under our sun shade protected from the wind until it was properly dry.

And so the days just flew by. Actually we were very lucky with the weather. Just shortly before New Year it got worse. It turned quite cool, the sky was full of clouds and there was such a strong wind that it became quite unbearable on the beach. If you weren't careful you'd get a gob full of sand. When it got like that, Vera was usually the only one left.

For Brenda and me that was just too much like hard work. We preferred to stay at home with a book, a video and a bit of light cookery. We weren't cooking the books of course (or the videos), but all the various different sorts of local vegetables that Brenda dragged home from the supermarket. Horse beans and French beans and those funny little roots that look like potatoes, and of course those dinky little potatoes that you have to boil up in sea water before you dip 'em in that red or green garlic sauce and eat 'em.

But one thing I simply have to tell you: bad weather can play havoc with a girl's figure. Somehow you always want whatever you haven't got in the house. Whenever Brenda got the bad weather munchies she'd rush into the kitchen and start opening and closing all the cupboards.

«Why on earth are you bangin' all them cupboard doors about?» I asked.

«Me? I'm not bangin' about at all.»

«Yes you are, I can 'ear ya! Are you lookin' for something?»

«No. What would I be lookin' for?»

«How am I s'posed to know? Are you hungry?»

«Oh, I don't really know. Are *you* hungry?»

«What's in the fridge then?»

«Nothing worth eatin'!»

«What about in the freezer?»

«No, there's nothing there. Only poppers!»

«Have we got any milk left?»

«Milk? Do you want me to make some custard then?»

«Well, maybe ...»

«I think we need to do some serious shopping again.»

«D'ya think so?»

«Oh, ya know what? I'll just run across the road and get some ice cream.»

«But I thought you wanted to lose weight.»

«Yes, I know. But we haven't eaten any ice cream all week.»

«OK, but don't buy one of them tiny packs again. They're such bad value for money.»

«Why don't you put the kettle on while I'm gone.»

«All right. But get some biscuits then for the tea.»

«OK, then I'd better get some more eggnogg as well.» This is what happened every time the weather was bad and we had to hang around in the apartment for hours.

We watched all the Bette Davis videos, and all the Barbra Streisand and Bette Midler films that any educated woman should be familiar with were there too. But watching all them films really makes a girl hungry. And that's why bad weather is such a killer for a girl's figure.

Actually I'm much more into epics myself you know, Ben Hur or that one where Moses and the children of Israel mince through the Red Sea with all them Egyptian pharaohs hot on their heels. I'm impressed by that. I can't walk on sand in heels, so Gawd knows how they got away! I love all them films. But I always had to watch them on my own in the living room while Brenda treated herself to something else upstairs. But as I was having a good old epic vada on New Year's Eve afternoon I could hear all sorts of banging and thumping going on. Somehow it really didn't go with the film at all.

«They know nothing about history in Hollywood do they?» I called upstairs to Brenda.

«What??» she called back down again.

«Well you tell me, the ancient Egyptians didn't have cannons and guns and stuff did they?»

«What on earth makes ya think that?»

«Well, Cleopatra's troops are supposed to be having a right old set-to with the Romans. But listen to all this shooting and banging!»

«Turn the sound off for a second.»

So I did just that, but the shooting and banging carried on.

«What the hell is that? Is it midnight already? I'm not going mad am I?» I wailed.

«But y' are, Blanche, y' are!» Brenda yelled back, and came trotting down the stairs. «No, it's not midnight, but the Spaniards obviously can't wait till it's dark. Sounds like the whole island's under attack. Oh, I can't concentrate on *Baby Jane* with all this goin' on. What shall we do tonight then?»

«Something easy and quiet,» I suggested. «Good food, good wine and good music. And then at New Year maybe we can pop into *Nestor's* for an hour or so.»

You see I generally prefer a quiet New Year myself. The other year we had a lovely time. We rented a cottage in the middle of the New Forest. It was ever so romantic and totally unhectic.

«Well I'm off to the gym for a start, and after that I'll go shoppin' and then we'll eat at nine,» said Brenda. And that's exactly what we did. Honestly, she was down that gym every day, regular as clockwork. «If you want a man, you've got to work for it. The natural look just ain't in any more, dear!» she would say, and shoot off to some trendy gym out near the *Faro 2 shopping centre* or somewhere like that. It makes me laugh because at home she wouldn't be seen dead within 200 metres of a gym. Lazy cow!

So once she'd gone, I scrubbed the house from top to bottom, and then myself, and then at half past four in spite of a light drizzle I trotted off to *Café Wien*. Honestly, it was like downtown Beirut on a busy night. At every street corner they were lettin' off bangers and shootin' rockets like there was no tomorrow. When I arrived at *Café Wien* my nerves were in shreds.

At first there wasn't a soul in there that I knew, so I just sat there on my own. But hardly had I ordered my apple tart with lashings of cream – delicious! – when in trolled the Queen Bee with her friend.

«You know, bad weather can be very tough on the credit cards,» she exclaimed, and spread out all her bags.

«What 'ave you been buying then?»

«Well, just the bare essentials a girl needs. I never find the time at home.»

«Well, did ya get perfume?»

«D'ya wanna have a smell?»

We were just testing the fourth bottle when the Brummies turned up. Bobette was all in a tizz again. «Hey Elvira, have you seen Sven?»

«Who's Sven?»

«You know, that Danish guy I was on the beach with yesterday.»

«I'm sorry, I really just can't keep track of all your Vikings!»

«Well! Are we catty today or what? I think you could do with de-clawing again!»

«Now what's that supposed to mean?»

«Ladies, please! Season of goodwill to all Marys, an' all that shit!» said the Queen Bee. «Why don't we all go out for dinner together tonight?»

«Go out for dinner? On New Year's Eve in Playa? Count me out. Wherever you go the food costs twice as much and tastes half as good. Rob and me are gonna cook something at home and then we can all meet up afterwards.»

I was just about to say how I hate these mass gatherings, they make me go all squiffy in the head, when all of a sudden there was a great roar over our heads.

«Take cover girls! We're under attack!» shrieked Bobette. And already the rocket was exploding over our heads. It gave me such a fright my cake fork flew right out of my hand.

«Really, these tired, phallic, macho war games really get on my tits!» screamed someone from the next table.

«Ooooh, I think I've split me kipper!»

«Really, how vulgar! I simply must have another piece of kipper tart. Did I say kipper tart? I mean apple tart.»

«I'm gonna pop over to *Marlene* and see if Sven's there.»

«Buy a bottle of bubbly on your way back for tonight, Bobby.»

It was all so hectic again. I really can't understand why it's always like that with the girls. As soon as half a dozen of them get together at one spot, off they go. And always at least one of 'em's having her period!

When I got home at half past six the stress continued. Jimbo was sitting there, that's my dream boy Philippe's other half, with Brenda on the couch and with a face like a wet wank in Wigan. He'd taken a few days more holiday than Philippe you see.

«What's up here? Has somebody died?»

«Oh, I just miss my Philippe sooo much,» Jimmy sighed, and poured himself another brandy.

«Then fly off after 'im!» I said.

«Now that's a bright idea, I never thought of that! What d'ya think I've been tryin' to do? Everything's full!» Brenda was obviously quite touched. Given half a chance she'd've started snivelling too. She always starts bawling anyway whenever there's an emotional scene. Shortly before Christmas when that tear-jerker ET was on the Spanish telly she sat in the living room with a swollen face mopping up the tears. Just because that ugly wrinkled little ET thing was homesick and kept pointing «mi casa, mi casa!» And then she called me a hardened cynical old queen coz I wouldn't cry along with 'er.

And now I was supposed to comfort Jemima! Well that really wasn't on. Who was comforting me? I mean after all, my Philippe-shaped wound wasn't healed yet either.

«I suppose I just have to deal with my pain on my own,» she finally said at about eight, and trolled off. Even though Brenda had asked her if she wanted to stay for dinner.

Luckily our New Year's Eve's dinner went off quite peacefully. Except of course for that nerve-racking din. Just as we were sitting comfortably with our coffee and brandies the Brummies dropped in with their bottle of bubbly.

«Let's down this quick and then shoot off to *Nestor's*. The party's well under way by now.»

«Let's wait till twelve,» said Brenda.

«Put the telly on. Let's see what the Spanish do on New Year's.»

There was some kind of *Hinge & Bracket* show on, and just as we were wondering what all the queenery was about Jemima came back. She was wearing dark trousers and a white jacket, had done her hair up all fresh, and looked like she was off to a royal garden party.

«D'ya think Philippe'll phone at midnight?»

«Of course!» said Brenda. «So we should wait here till twelve.»

But just before eleven the tranny show suddenly ended and they were showing the Prado clock or whatever that thing is and all Madrid was celebrating New Year.

«Are they mad?» shrieked Roberta. «My watch only says eleven.» But then we remembered that we were an hour behind mainland Spain in the Canaries.

«Let's toast the New Year now,» said Bobette.

«Let's wait another hour, I'm sure Philippe'll call then!» cried Brenda in a funny sort of voice.

I realised that I was teetering on the edge of a crisis again, and so I opened the bottle of bubbly, we all clinked our glasses, and then the Brummies shot off to *Nestor's*.

It was odd though, like we were in limbo between two years. The old one was gone but the new one hadn't started yet, and Philippe hadn't phoned. Brenda was still sitting in her armchair, which wasn't like her. Jemima was staring disconsolately at the telephone and I couldn't help thinking about the New Forest, and just occasionally about Philippe.

All of a sudden I couldn't take it any more. «Well I'm goin' to *Nestor's* as well.»

«I'll come too,» said Jemima.

«Go on then!» exclaimed Brenda, and showed no signs of shifting her arse off that armchair.

«Are you really gonna stay here all on yer own?»

«Yeees!»

«Don't ya think that's a bit odd?»

«Nooo!»

«Are you sure you're all right?»

«Of course. I'll catch you up later.»

«What's up with Brenda?» asked Jemima as I was locking the garden gate.

«Oh, she's just havin' a funny five minutes.»

*Nestor's* of course was packed to the rafters. Thousands of queens all crushed into one spot and then all the explosions in the air and on the ground. And by this time there were so many people we knew there. Everyone was chatting over one another's heads across the room, saying hello here and kissing one another there, and some even had paper hats and red noses on, and needless to say everybody was wishing everybody else a *Happy New Year*.

But then Jemima started up again. «Oh, I'm so terribly upset.»

«Really?»

«D'you think Philippe is thinking about me now?»

«I'm sure he is. Can't you feel it?»

«Oh, I don't know. Everyone's trying to talk me out of being upset but I'm just being honest about it.»

«I'd be honest about it too. But it's not me Philippe's in love with, is it?»

«What d'ya mean? Have you slept with 'im then?»

«No! I'm just sayin' ...»

«Oh, I see.»

«Hey, what d'ya think Brendan's up to now?» it suddenly occurred to Jemima.

«He's probably thinking about you the whole time,» I answered automatically.

«Brendan? Why me?»

«Oh, Brenda? She'll still be moping about at home.»

«D'you think he's done something to himself?»

Now I don't know what you would've done if you'd had to spend the first hours of the New Year comforting the wife of your dream man.

«You know what, I'll just pop over and 'ave a look and see what she's up to,» I said, and just rushed off.

When I got to the house at first I got a small shock. In the living room all the lights and the telly were on and there was no sign of Brenda at all. When I went up the stairs and stopped outside her bedroom door I could hear voices as if there was a party going on in there. Did she have visitors? Had she organised a New Year's orgy behind my back? Group sex? I thought, and listened carefully at the door. But then my curiosity got the better of me and I opened it. Because I recognised two of the voices. It was Michael Caine and Julie Walters! And Brenda giggling away like a madwoman in between. She was lying there, totally in her element, snuggled up in bed with a bottle of bubbly and a box of dried dates, staring at the telly and shaking with laughter.

«Aaahh, that's sooo funny! That Rita is such a laugh!»

«Well, that's nice. And you leave me to stagger into the New Year with that whinging Jemima?»

«Well, you could've waited another hour!»

«Why?»

«Well, fifteen minutes ago Philippe phoned from England and very sweetly wished me a *Happy New Year*.»

«You?! I don't believe it!»

«And Jim as well, of course.»

«And what about me?»

«No. I s'pose he musta forgotten you.»

Well, what can you say to that? I sacrifice myself to stop his wife flinging herself into the Atlantic – and then that!

This New Year really was a complete waste of time. This'd never have happened to me on a romantic quiet night in the New Forest!

### The Traces on the Ground, That Yesterday I found, Or: These terrible farewell scenes really take it out of you!

In Playa you see these terrible, heartbreaking farewell scenes every day of the week. And they really do take it out of you, you know. You honestly can't imagine the dreadful tragedies that happen there. And all for love! She's such a fickle mistress ain't she? What she gives with one hand she takes with the other! Ooh, that was very Shakespearean, wasn't it?!?

For example, that guide dog chappy from Glasgow. On her last day she was stood in *Mykonos* in a total state, clutching her little treasure from the Spanish mainland close to her bosom. As she was so small and the Glaswegian so big she had to climb up onto a bar-stool to even reach his neck with her little arms.

«Oh look, they're doing that koala bear routine again!» said Vera, quite out of place. She has absolutely no respect for the power of love!

I mean, it's really something quite wonderful when two people love each other so much that they burst into tears when they have to say goodbye. But those two were actually quite lucky. At least they arrived together and left together. Even if they did go off to quite different destinations.

It's much worse if you're left behind as a widow! That's what happened to my dear friend Gracie from Stockport. She was flown in shortly before New Year's and wham, within seconds she'd fallen in love with Wolfgang. He came from some picturesque little village near Munich and was more than half way through his holiday. And so they only had a few days to enjoy their happiness. And when they were over … it was one hellova drama!

I even went with Gracie to the airport coz I knew she'd have a total breakdown when Wolfgang's plane took off. And so it was of course. So I took her to Sioux City so that the Mistress of the Knives could take her mind off things.

Oh sorry, I haven't introduced you to the Mistress of the Knives yet have I? Well, never mind. I'll tell you that story in a bit.

But the trip to Sioux City didn't help one bit. Gracie was in a dreadful state. «Wolfgang is the love of my life,» she kept sobbing. «I'm going to Bavaria. Even if I 'ave to spend the rest o' me life runnin' around in them lederhosen. I just don't care.»

«Maybe you should take up the tuba so you can play in one o' them brass bands,» I said to try and take her mind off it. But she wasn't havin' it.

«Oh I can't stand all that Oompah-Oompah rubbish!»

«But you've got to do something to occupy yourself dear! How about brewing beer? They're very hot on that in Bavaria.»

«That's great. But where am I gonna get me hands on a sack of hops here in Playa?»

Now, there's no answer to that one. So Gracie just spent all the next day on her sun lounger with her Walkman on in a world of her own. Now, it was all right as long as she kept her pain to herself, but once she started to sing along with the Walkman, we all understood perfectly what she was putting herself through:

> *The traces on the ground*
> *That yesterday I found,*
> *The rain has washed away,*
> *What's left for me today?*
> *Lalalaaa lala*
> *Lalalaaa lala*
> *The rain has washed away ...»*

Now this kind of song can be a harbour in a storm. It can also be a pain in the arse! To begin with, Gracie just quietly hummed along the chorus: «Lalalaaa lala.»

But each time the song ended she'd wind the tape back to the beginning and the sobbing would start all over again.

«I think we should call the Red Cross,» said Brenda. «She's workin' 'erself into a frenzy!»

«Don't be daft! She's just working through 'er pain. Things like this take time, that's all.»

But then Gracie started to sing along to all the lyrics. Now I wouldn't mind normally, but she's got a voice like a cat going through a mangle. Of course a girl can't put up with that for more than an hour or so – your nerves are just shot to pieces!

The English ladies were remarkably controlled with their protests. Stiff upper lip an' all that. The Dutch girls were the first to crack. «Can't you switch her off? Just take the Walkman off the stupid cow! I think I'm gonna be sick! We'll be demanding compensation from Tony Blair!» they kept shouting.

Then the Swedes started throwing empty Coke cans at Gracie. I mean, really! That just wasn't on. Attacking a poor, suffering woman like that. I gave them a good tongue-lashing and they stopped it. But then they started calling me Thatcher's daughter! The things a girl has to go through on her hols!

At last I went over to Gracie and advised her to retreat a couple of hundred metres back into the dunes and sing there. She did, and harmony was restored once more.

It took three whole days until she'd recovered enough to even think of looking at another man. And that was where The Mistress of the Knives from Sioux City comes in. You see, this was her great romance from her last Playa holiday, and she started twisting Gracie around her little finger.

«Just good friends, o' course!» she said, and then went charging off to Sioux City every day to watch The Mistress of the

Knives at work. By the way, her real name was Alfonso. So once I went along too.

Well this Alfonsina really was quite an impressive-looking number. For many long and bitter years she'd worked as a tomato-picker-woman and had gradually taught herself to throw knives.

«Yes, I just took along a dozen knives, put the basket for the tomatoes under the bush, and began throwing the knives at the stalks. Of course, to begin with there was a lot of ketchup all over the place, but after a while I got the hang of it.»

And then, when she'd got really good at it, she stopped practising on tomatoes but – and you'll never believe this -started on her own mother instead.

Where there's a will there's a way. And they wanted to get away from the Ketchup Fields. Apparently Alfonsina said to her mother: «Mummy dearest, I just can't stand these stupid tomatoes any more. I, your daughter, was born to higher things. Come with me. We're sure to find something better than tomatoes any day.» And so the two of them turned their backs on ketchup, packed up their things and moved to Sioux City. And that's where I saw Alfonsina at work with me very own eyes. She really did tie her own mother onto one of them wooden wheel thingies and then gave a good push so that it spun round. The wheel that is, but the mother too of course coz she was strapped to it. And then the knives began to fly!

I didn't even dare gasp for fear that Alfonsina might lose her concentration and carve her dear old mum up good and proper!

«I think you should reconsider that Bavaria business,» I said to Gracie. «If her mother can survive this madness, I'm sure you could as well. And at least the weather is better here than in some tiny Bavarian shithole.»

«Oh, I don't know though. Queens and their mothers! I'd rather not get involved.»

«Maybe you could go on the wheel with the mother?»

«What? D'ya think I'm mad? Just imagine if I had a marriage crisis with Alfonso! And then had to hang around on that there wheel? What if he chose his mother over me? I'd end up with a dagger in me guts! I'm not stupid, dear.»

«Then you'll just 'ave to pull yourself together, won't you!»

But there was no reasoning with Gracie. She'd got her heart set on Bavaria. And then she had to comfort The Mistress of The Knives. I thought that was really nice of her though!

Well, you help wherever you can, don't you? Even I, with my extremely thin knowledge of the French language, couldn't help myself when Trixie was struck with sorrow in the shape of a Brussels sprout. Now Trixie came from Swindon and was a «top pedagogical manager, practising in the Health Service». Well, that's what she always used to say anyway. She taught nursing at a large hospital. Some girls really do come up with the most bizarre rubbish to try and improve their image.

At any rate, Trixie was a nurse and had this Belgian lover called Marcel. He looked very interesting, somehow tasteful. But he didn't speak a word of English and Trixie didn't speak a word of French. Of course at first they just shagged all day like rabbits, but when the sperm finally ran out they had to talk to each other!

«Veux-tu un drink?» Marcel asked Trixie in *Nestor's*.

«What did he say, Elvira?»

«D'ya wanna a drink?»

«Tell 'im, yes please.»

«Oui, Trixie veut,» I said.

«Merci,» Trixie said then. «Ask 'im how long he's stayin' in Playa.»

«À Playa, combien de jours veux-tu rester ici?» I said. And then Marcel came out with such a long answer that I didn't understand a single word.

«What did he say, Elvira?»

«I haven't a clue, he spoke too fast.»

«Then tell 'im to speak more slowly.»

«I don't know what slowly is in Belgian.»

«Plus lent,» chipped in a kindly gal at the next table. «Oh, could you carry on translating here for a while. I simply have to dash to the loo!» I said, and just left 'em to it.

And so their affair lasted for all of two days. It was just too much like hard work. On the third day Trixie was walking along the beach, obviously sad but somehow quite composed. And she was quietly singing that comforting little melody by Françoise Hardy:

> *Ask the silver moon*
> *Where love lies*
> *But don't ask it*
> *Why it sometimes dies.*

Now if she'd have asked me instead of the silver moon I could have told her! It's because she's crap at languages of course! But nowadays the girls don't really want to get too deep into why it all went wrong, in case they find out it's them.

Everything is blurring in front of my eyes. It's so awful! I just can't go on writing. I think I'm having a flashback! Yes, that's it ...

It's all coming back to me. The terrible grief, the sorrow. I just heard on the radio that today, the 7th May, is the anniversary of Marlene Dietrich's death. I remember it vividly. I was in shock for days and had to have a week of official mourning. I just couldn't believe it, Marlene gone! Apparently she passed away at three o'clock in the afternoon. Reading a book, in her armchair. She was buried in Berlin. I think queens from all over the world should get together and see to it that the grave is permanently covered with heaps of fresh red roses. Apparently she could be a bit funny about girls like us, but nevertheles, I think she did her bit to save us all from the Nazis. I mean, after all, she did troll about at the front and keep the Yanks happy and in good fighting spirits with her songs.

But I must say I thought all them obituaries that came out about her were really stupid. They kept going on about the death of a legend. I mean, what a load of rubbish! The legend didn't die! It lives on. We'll see to that, won't we? Just like Vera Lynn. She never really died either, did she?

But there are some people who are well dead and buried in my book even though they're still alive. Apparently some people refused to go to Marlene's funeral coz they said she'd betrayed her fatherland. Really! They should bring back public birching for idiots like that!

Now where was I? Oh yes, back to Playa! I was tellin' you about Trixie wasn't I? Now she was a one. We were always having to comfort her. You see she'd come on holiday with her ex-husband, Angie, and was staying with him in the same apartment. They were at each other all the time.

«It's so awful! I think I'm gonna end up killin' 'im,» Trixie kept complaining.

«Why don't ya just split up properly, once and for all? Better a terrible end than endless terror, dear!»

«Yes, well, I've been on the lookout for a replacement now for ages. But I just haven't found anything suitable.»

«Oh, and that's why you stay with your ex is it?»

«Of course! A bird in the hand's worth two in the bush. Keep hold and keep looking, that's my motto.»

Well really, some of the tactics girls come up with nowadays! I would never've dreamt of such an idea. It was just like hetero hell!

«And how long's this been goin' on for?»

«Oh, about seven or eight years now,» said Trixie. *«I haven't made it easy, I've often asked myself, Is it love that's in the air, Or just pigeon shit in me hair?»*

99

«Well, ya know what Trixie? *Whoever seeketh love, Love he must also give, Must learn to understand, And often to forgive.*»

«You're telling me. Now I always thought it was: *The Things That Dreams Are Made Of,* until I found *That Ole Devil Called Love* in bed with another man and then it was *Good Morning Heartache.*

Now of course that's not an easy thing for a girl to put up with. But then it's usually just when you expect it the least that love comes a-calling. That's what happened to me anyway. And it all began with a dead rabbit. You see Brenda decided she wanted a good old-fashioned rustic dinner. And so we jumped on the bus and headed outta Playa. Quite a way in fact towards Puerto de Mogan, and in a quaint coastal village we found a cosy little restaurant.

«I need something wild today,» she said, and ordered herself a rabbit. And I had a steak with all the trimmings. And I must say it was delicious. But Brenda didn't seem to be having so much luck with 'er bunny. She kept just pickin' and pokin' about at it.

«Don't ya like it?»

«Oh, I've certainly had better rabbit before.»

«Well, I s'pose it does look a bit thin.»

«Say, have you noticed anything funny 'ere?»

«No. What d'ya mean?»

«Well, usually in these types of idyllic little restaurants there's always lots o' cats runnin' about ain't there?»

So I had a good look round but I couldn't see any either.

«Funny innit?» I said, and had a better look at the dead creature on Brenda's plate. «Rabbitwise it looks quite normal.»

«Yes, well 'ave a look at it catwise. It looks quite normal then an' all!»

And just as we were debating this thorny problem a little further, two very interesting-looking numbers came into the restaurant and sat down at the next table.

You know how these things go: I just glanced over every now and then, and after a while I noticed that one of 'em kept smiling back at me in a very friendly way. The way he did it, there was something really special about it, I just couldn't help smiling back.

«Well, I'm not gonna eat it!» said Brenda. «Jugged hare? I might just as well've ordered rat in a hat! 'Ere, are you even listening to me?»

Of course Brenda had noticed straight away that something was going on, and quite unabashedly turned around to get a good view. I always find that sort of thing so embarrassing, coz then the other lot immediately know they're being talked about.

«Looks good! You'd better hurry up and land yer catch, girl!»

But it wasn't as easy as that coz we had to catch the bus back and it went in twenty minutes.

«How can I strike up a conversation with 'im?» I asked in despair.

«Walk past their table and drop yer handkerchief. That always worked for Marilyn Monroe.»

«Aren't you mixing 'er up with Ingrid Bergmann?»

«I dunno, maybe.»

«D'ya think it'll work with a Kleenex?»

«Looks a bit cheap don't it?»

In any case it didn't work at all and there was me sitting totally frustrated in the bus back to Playa. «Next time we go there we have to rent a car.»

«You won't catch me going back there in a hurry duckie! But we should think about renting a car soon anyway. Then we can do a tour around the island. The Brummies want to come along as well.»

«We're bound to see them tonight in *Mykonos*.»

«Yes, and then we can make arrangements.»

Well, later on as we were standing around in *Mykonos* passing the time of day who should come trolling in? – my chap from the restaurant – all on his own. I was in seventh heaven!

«Eh, he's looking for you!»

And so he was. Inside of five minutes I'd found out his name was Martin, that he actually came from Richmond but had moved to Coventry for his new job, was on holiday in Playa for two weeks staying at the *Lenamar*, and was leaving on Saturday.

We hadn't been chatting very long when he started kissing me and said: «Your place or mine?»

Now actually that was all a bit fast for me. But it was the usual dilemma: if you say something evasive you don't know if he'll stay on the hook, and if you go for it straight away you don't know if you're gonna end up with the rabbit or the cat!

But actually I was still very keen on Martin. And after all that snogging I started thinking with me willy instead of with me brain.

«Let's go to my place,» I said, coz it was nearer. And so that's what we did. But first of all we just kissed and cuddled in the garden under the palm trees. The night was so lovely and mild.

«You know, an open-air performance can be quite fun,» said Martin after a while. «But actually I would prefer a real bed!»

«D'ya wanna drink?» I asked when we were in the living room. But by that time it was too late for drinks: Mother Nature demanded her rights, she just couldn't be stopped! So we went straight up to my bedroom and the action began.

Naked in bed is always the most fun I think, don't you? Now if you think I'm gonna give you all the gory details I'm afraid you've got another think coming!

At any rate we left out the Russian Roulette and kept it all *safe and beautiful*. But after about two hours we were completely shagged out. And then it got a bit tricky.

Of course when you're done it's always fab to cuddle up together completely exhausted and fall asleep. But it ain't comfy! Particularly when you've become such an expert at sleeping alone after so many long lonely nights practising.

You know, legs wrapped around each other, lower bodies pressed together coz it's so nice to feel his knob against you, upper bodies on their sides, his head on one of my arms, my mouth against his neck, his arms kinda on my back and my other arm around his shoulders.

Get the picture? Good. But what I'm sure you can't picture is how Martin snored. I thought I was gonna get concussion!

It's always the same. The guys I cop off with always fall asleep so quick after. It's so insensitive, so nafflike. How they always manage it is a mystery to me. And then you just lie there for hours wondering, «What are you doing?»

Now, you don't want to be impolite when you've got visitors, do you? But the deeper Martin slept the louder he thundered into my right ear. You really can't stick it for long. So I just freed myself from that knot of legs and arms, turned my back on him, and stuffed little balls of chewed-up bog paper in my lug 'oles. I find that's so much better than earplugs, don't you? It doesn't keep falling out. And that helped a bit. As soon as I'd got the bog roll in, Martin stopped snoring. But not for long. He must've noticed that I somehow wasn't there any more and hey presto he came shuffling over, wrapped his arm around my shoulders and within seconds was bellowing into my other ear.

When you're lying there wide-awake in bed that's when regret comes a-calling. If only you'd gone back with him to *Lenamar*! It's only a couple of hundred yards up the *Avenida*. Then you could just grab your clothes and go home. But no! Bloody hormones! That's what you get for givin' in to yer chemical urges!

At about four I heard Brenda come home. What on earth will she think? I thought. She'll think we're sawing the bed in half or the wardrobe or something. Or she'll be giggling, enjoying every minute of it, thinking: how can Elvira put up with that? She's usually so sensitive to noise. And in fact it's true. It's incredible the stress and strain that the old sex drive puts us through.

At about six I must've fallen asleep at least for a bit. Coz Martin woke me up when he staggered out for a pee. But after about half an hour he still hadn't come back. Has he fallen asleep on the bog, I wondered, and popped in to check on him. I carefully pulled open the sliding door to the bathroom but he wasn't there. Has he snuck off home? Without 'is drag? Coz that was still strewn all over the bedroom floor. As I tiptoed down to the living room I spied him quite peacefully kipping on the sofa. Oh, that's good, I thought, and brought him some blankets down to keep his tootsies warm, at least I can get some decent shut-eye now without that frightful snoring. After three and a half hours, at nine thirty, I woke up again to the sound of Brenda shaving in the bathroom – for hours. She's not pulling each hair out individually I hope? Has she gone completely mad? I thought, and really couldn't work out what on earth was going on.

But then Martin came back into the bedroom. «I just wanted to see what the business with the electric razor was all about,» he said all sleepily, and cuddled up to me again.

«Brendan must've grown bristles over night,» I assumed.

«Well, as long as you haven't grown bristles,» he replied, and so a repeat performance of the night before's show piece got underway!

«Why did you go down to the living room to sleep?» I asked him afterwards.

«Well, you know, I'm awfully sorry, but I'm very sensitive to snoring.»

«What? *Me?* Did I snore?»

«You never really hear your own snoring properly.»

«You're telling me!» I said. «Must be because I was concussed by yours!»

Despite the thunderous night, my concussion wasn't so bad that I couldn't make the breakfast. But when I went downstairs I found a note from Brenda: «Gone to Las Palmas. Be back around *Nestor* time.» So I knew she wouldn't be later than around half ten.

As the weather was really very good, Martin and I went back to his apartment, picked up his beach things and round about lunch time waddled off to the sea. «I usually go to the beach earlier,» I said, as we strode through that particular part of the dunes, Bongoland.

«Yes, me too.»

«These by-ways are pretty dead at this time of day aren't they?»

«Yes, you're right. I can't see any hungry morning Bongos trolling around.»

«There are more evening Bongos than morning Bongos in these parts anyway.»

«Oh I dunno though,» he replied. «My friend John from Putney is a morning Bongo. He always rushes off to catch the morning sun, he says to me.»

«But most of them rush off to catch the evening sun, so they always say anyway,» I said.

«That's probably more practical too. Then at least they can say they had to stay behind to lock up the dunes.»

«I think I'll have to ask Lucy about that one. She generally knows everything.»

«Who's Lucy then?»

«Don't ya know *Lucy in the Sky*? She's a quite adorable academic. For the last ten days she's been in the front row and reads at least three scientific volumes on homosexuality per day.»

«D'ya think the numerical relation between morning and evening Bongos is in them somewhere then?»

«Oh no, I shouldn't think so, not yet.»

«Maybe it's genuine academic virgin territory. Perhaps some

gay scientist'll do some big research project on it soon. What d'ya think?»

«Naah, I don't think so.»

«Why not?»

«They'd have to mingle with the Bongos and take tallies.»

«D'ya think proper scientists wouldn't be allowed to coz they'd have to keep an objective distance from the real gay scene, or what?»

«Mmm, I s'pose so.»

«But they must have to want to get a bit involved. Then they could combine research and practice.»

«Maybe they're not as 'involved' as your regular gay men.»

«Oh, look over there. There's someone sitting in that tree waving over to us with 'is stiffy,» Martin suddenly said.

«Really, I've never seen a genuine tree bongo before.»

«Just look at that, how 'involved' he is. He's almost falling off 'is branch!»

«Gays are apparently much more sex-driven than naffs anyway.»

«Where did you get that from?»

«Oh some critical gay sexpert wrote it once. She even went so far as to say: The process of heterosexualisation is the road to sexual barrenness.»

«How can she say that? Maybe the process of homosexualisation is something like a process of turning into a sexual zombie.»

«It certainly looks that way sometimes.»

When we finally got to the gay beach all the sun loungers in the front rows were taken. But quite near the back we found ourselves a nice little spot.

The sun was shining so warm, everything was so peaceful, and after we'd had a good old splash about in the waves I noticed I was beginning to fall just a wee bit in love with Martin.

He lay there quite relaxed on his sun lounger, and coz he

liked it so much I fondled the hair on the back of his head for him. After a while though it became very obvious just how much he liked it. And just as he was turning over to lie on his stomach someone behind us suddenly bawled out: «It's disgusting! Aren't you at all ashamed of yourselves? These damned homo-seck-shoo-ells are quite unbearable! Wherever you go you can't get away from them. Why can't you just disappear?»

«Walter! Don't get all worked up,» his missus tried to calm him down.

«Be quiet Margaret! What filth! We shouldn't have to put up with it. This riff-raff's getting more and more outrageous. Come on Margaret. Pack up your things. We're going somewhere else.»

Well, we were at a loss for words. They were naffs that had wandered into the gay section.

«Why don't you just disappear – up your own arseholes! This part of the beach is gay and is staying gay, you ... you ...» shouted Martin in such a rage that he couldn't think of an appropriate insult.

«You stupid hetero terrorist!» somebody behind us kindly finished his sentence for him.

«Exactly. These naffs think they own the whole world,» someone yelled across from nearby.

«Well, if you must insist on playing tonsil tennis in public like that what do you expect? You just don't do things like that in public,» somebody hollered over from the other side.

«We weren't playing tonsil tennis in public!» I shouted back.

«I saw it!» he called back.

«Wishful thinking more like! There wasn't anything to see.» Martin was really mad at the old cow now. All of a sudden everyone around us had got all excited and was bitching all over the place.

«Well, the naffs 've got enough room of their own. They've

got no business sticking their noses in here. It's gay here and that's the way it's gonna stay.»

«Even so, people can still behave decently!» the cow mooed again.

«What's wrong with him stroking his boyfriend's hair?»

«Yes, the naffs just have to accept that.»

«They touch each other too, don't they!»

«That's different.»

«How come?»

«Well, they're normal.» That really got things going.

«What on earth is normal then? Aren't you normal? Or what are you?»

«I'm just different.»

«I see, you're not gay, you're just different, is that it?»

«Oh, I'm not havin' that. I won't stand for insults like that from a queen like you!»

«Don't call me a queen!»

«Stop it girls!» someone suddenly shouted, «can't you just all calm down and be friends?»

«When you say 'girls' like that it really makes me feel sick.»

«Oh pull yourself together. Don't forget you don't want all the naffs coming down here either.»

«That wouldn't bother me. I'm tolerant!»

«He's just plain stupid,» Martin whispered in my ear, «he can't be tolerant as well.»

«Then why don't you go over to the naffs' beach then?» someone called over to the stupid one.

«I'm not having you dictate to me where I can go on the beach thank you.»

«We really should think of ways to stand up to these naffs. After all, there's more and more of them coming to our part of the beach every day. I can hardly be myself here anymore,» I heard someone over to the side saying.

«Well, I think we should set up a discussion group to exchange experiences. I mean, we haven't all had the same experience with straights. After all, my mother was straight too.»

«How d'ya know? I bet she had a lesbian side to her an' all.»

«Oh no, not 'er. She's hardcore hetero.»

«I think if we want to get rid of the naffs all we have to do is really camp it up all the time. Then they'll go away of their own accord.»

«Rubbish! They watch Lily on the telly don't they? She camps it up and that doesn't put them off.»

«Exactly! You see, the naffs try'n monopolise everything. They can't even leave camping up to us! Gay oppression is getting worse and worse!»

«I think I'm going mad!» Martin groaned, fell like a stone down onto his sun lounger, and pulled his beach towel over his head in exasperation.

«I can't watch this misery any longer.»

«Well, that's no good! You can still hear it all,» I said, pulled the towel off his head, and gave him a quick kiss.

«The naffs here do bother me though really,» he carried on moaning. «Either they stare at you like animals in a zoo or they're just downright rude. We really shouldn't have to put up with it.»

«I think this part of the beach should stay gay too. The next bit just over there is much more mixed. You've got your usual lesbians and gay men, a few bisexuals, even some straights, and of course the closet cases,» I agreed with him.

«That's where I've been for the last few days. The guy I'm on holiday with doesn't dare come over here.»

«Is there anything going on between you two?»

«Nah, we're just good friends. There's never been anything between us.»

«And why doesn't he dare come over here?»

Martin sat up again, blinked a bit embarrassed against the sun, and then bent down to me again.

«Maybe he's afraid that someone he knows might see him.»

«And what about you? Aren't you afraid?»

«Not when I've got a lover I can trust,» he answered, and went all red.

«Well, strength in unity,» I said after a while.

«That was lovely, the way you said that. Like a fortune teller in her tent at the fair!»

«Cheeky git!»

«The valley of darkness hasn't been completely crossed after all!» Martin sat back up and watched the continuing goings-on.

«We could install sentries on both sides of the gay beach,» someone suggested.

«Oh yes, and they could let the cute naffboys in and keep the ugly ones out!»

«You've got a one-track mind!»

«The straight men should stay out, but the women can come in!»

«What makes ya say that?»

«They could be lesbians. Or just straight women that know they don't 'ave to worry about gettin' bothered by men.»

«Oh, bog off and take yer lesbians with ya! They won't let us in their bars, so why should we let 'em on our beach? Don't be daft!»

«Right. They always jump on our bandwagon and expect us to fight their battles for them. And then when they feel strong enough they turn on us and say: We always knew, you gays are just a load of oppressive men too!»

«I think you're rather simplifying the issue.»

«Oh, all the lesbians I know have no sense of humour and are always grumpy. Basically they're machos!»

«The ones I know aren't like that.»

«We could put up warning signs at each end of the gay beach.»

«And what should they say?»

«Well, *Piss Off Naffs!* of course!»

«Oh, you're loopy you are.»

«I'd find a sign like that quite oppressive.»

«Exactly! That somehow reminds me of Adolf Hitler.»

«Oh, you silly thing you! You're getting mixed up with Max Bygraves, he's dead as well!»

«In what language should we write it then?»

Suddenly Martin leapt up and pulled on his trunks. «I'm going to the kiosk to get an ice cream. D'ya want anything?»

«I'll come with ya. By the time they've come to a decision here we'll be back anyway.»

And so it was. Although the sun wasn't shining quite as warm and the wind was gradually getting colder, the jabbering still went on and on.

But as I looked around at the sun loungers on the gay beach I saw that it was getting emptier and emptier. Even Lucy had closed her book, packed up her library and was gone. It'd really got quite cool and the second silent bell for *Marlene's* was already ringing its little head off.

«Just look at that!» someone shouted quite outraged.

«We're breaking our backs fighting for gay rights and all these queers just run off to the clubs and couldn't give a shit about the struggle!»

«Exactly! These consumer queens are only interested in consumption.»

«There! You see just how apolitical they are.»

«Let's just get on with it.»

I pulled on me sweatshirt coz with that cold wind it'd really got quite chilly.

«Come on, let's go too,» said Martin all of a sudden. «These wankers are really getting on my nerves.»

«Shall we go to *Marlene's* or to *Wien*, or d'ya wanna go somewhere else?»

«Let's just stroll down the beach to Maspalomas and then get the bus back home.»

«Great,» I thought.

We got dressed, packed up our stuff, and walked across the sand that was still warm down to the water.

For a while we just stared silently out to sea. The tide was coming in and the wind was blowing a shallow swell over the flat beach.

Martin sat down on an abandoned sun lounger and rubbed the sand from his feet.

«How long have you been gay?» he asked me unexpectedly as he was putting on his socks and trainers.

«Always. And you?»

We set off along the beach.

«I s'pose I always have been too. But I only really came to terms with it a few years ago.»

«Did someone wake you with a kiss, Sleeping Beauty?»

«Something like that I s'pose. With me it took a hellova long time. First I had to get over the hetero in me before I could find my true self.»

«And how did you do that? Stabbed him, drowned him, strangled him, poisoned him?»

«No, I just said: I don't want you. Piss off. I want to be myself.»

«And since then you can't stand the sight of straights?»

He laughed and stood still. «You mean because of just then, because I reacted so strongly.»

I stopped too and nodded.

He stood with his back to the water. The late afternoon sun was shining in his face. «If a guy like that is rude to us just because we touch each other then you can't just keep your mouth shut. It's a question of self-respect. You have to do something about it.»

I looked into his eyes and then at the foaming crowns of the waves as they glided in to the beach from far away. «You're right,» I said.

«It took far too long before I dared to say 'I love you' to another man. I've learnt here in Playa that there are many different types of gay men, and that you can talk to them and not just sleep with them. That has helped me find my way, make friends and get a grasp of my life in a small town. But that's not enough, because ...» he stopped in mid-sentence.

From the direction we were going came someone I knew walking towards us. Shortly before he reached us he slowed his pace without stopping. «So, 'ave ya found yerself a new man?» he called over to me. «Don't look too bad. But not as good as t' other one you were hangin' around with in *Nestor's* t'other day.»

The guy grinned wickedly, tossed his head back and walked away across the damp sand in the other direction.

«Who was that cow?» asked Martin.

«Angie. But that won't mean anything to you.»

«Why does he go and do something like that?»

I shrugged my shoulders. «Spitefulness is a kind of survival mechanism too. Maybe some sort of self-defence.»

«But he wanted to hurt us.»

«Me more like. He doesn't know you.»

«He wanted to hurt me too.»

«Don't take it so hard.» I wrapped my arm around his shoulders.

We continued along the beach and came to those big flat stones that lie on the sand just before Maspalomas. The waves were washing around the lower ones, but the higher ones were dry. I sat down, scratched a bit of tar off the sole of my foot, and waited till a wave came and washed the sand from my feet. Martin watched me silently while I put my socks and trainers on my wet feet. «Ready?»

When I looked at him again I found his features even more

attractive than before. He felt my attraction, put his arm around my waist and hooked his thumb through one of the belt loops in my jeans and smiled at me slightly embarrassed.

«Actually I still am a little bit afraid to act openly gay in public.»

«You never really know how people will react to it.»

«Before I was really gay I read a lot about homosexuality in books. Mostly scientific stuff, you know. And guess what was missing the most for me?»

«Well?»

«An answer to the question of why there is so little solidarity between gays.»

«How d'ya mean?»

«We gays are a minority that has suffered a great deal in society – we should stick together much more, secure the freedoms we've gained, consolidate our liberation. But usually we do exactly the opposite. Most of 'em spend more time trying to destroy each other than trying to achieve something together.»

«Well, the girls are world champions at that!»

«D'ya think that's good?»

«Not really ...» I replied somewhat embarrassed.

«I once read the sentence: 'nobody is gay without being punished somehow'. I think often the punishment for being gay is handed out by gay men themselves.»

«D'ya think so? But gay men are also individuals, you can't change that.»

«Even individuals have common interests. Why is it that gay men of all people are incapable of perceiving them?»

«Ask me something easier.»

«It's all about looking out for each other. If a queen gets beaten up somewhere, the others all run away. If a politician says something nasty about gays, they just all close their ears. If there's something wicked in the paper, they just don't read it. And when some naff's rude to us, then we just argue amongst ourselves like a load of mental cases. And then some bitch like Angie comes trolling down the beach spitting poison. You can't tell me all of that's normal. Tell that Lucy she should do some scientific research into this abnormal behaviour.»

«Now you've really got going!»

He laughed and pulled his thumb out of my jeans. «Okay, then I'll just jump into the water and cool myself down again.»

«For heavan's sake. You'll catch your death. It's far too cold for that now. Stay here!»

«Oh get out of it!» he shouted, and was already half undressed. «The waves'll warm me up.»

So I just squatted on the beach like Zoe the lesbian in *Survivor* and watched Martin splashing about all on his own in the water.

Now I couldn't do that. If I'm all on my own in the sea I can't help feeling strangely scared. I mean, you never really know what's in there do you?

But I got his towel out ready and when he came out of the water freezing I rubbed him dry.

«So, do you think you're ready to look out for someone then?» he asked, and looked deep into my eyes.

«For you, any time!» I was surprised by how easily I said that.

We kissed for quite a while.

«Shall we take a tour around the island tomorrow? Just you and me.»

I nodded.

He got dressed. We carried on along the beach in silence. As we reached the restaurants on the promenade the smell of cooking meat wafted towards us. I noticed Martin sniffing.

«Hungry?» I asked.

«Yes, pretty.»

«Let's go over to *Stairway* and get something to eat.» We spent the whole evening in Maspalomas, watched the surfers coming in with their surfboards, the sun go down, talked and laughed a lot, and went back to Playa on the bus in the dark. First of all though we made arrangements to spend the night together in *Lenamar*.

«See you later then.» I waved to him on the bus as he had to get off one stop later.

My watch said half past eleven. It'd been *Nestor* time for at least an hour. I crossed the Avenida and went down the passage to the cafe. It was bursting at the seams and there, right in the thick of it, sat Brenda.

«Where've you been?» she asked as she saw me come charging in with my beach bag.

«On the beach of course.»

«This late? I hope you put on plenty of anti-freeze!»

Then we filled each other in with all the details of what'd happened all day and what I'd done with Martin. But in spite of all that I immediately noticed why Brenda'd taken so long shaving.

«What on earth happened to you?» I asked quite shocked.

«So what? It's much more practical like this.»

She'd cut her hair real short.

«Come on. Are you mad? You look like a slave trader.»

«So? When you've got hair as thin as mine you 'ave to do this every now and again. Then it grows better.»

«And what about all the SM freaks on the island? Word'll get around that a new and unknown mistress has flown in.»

«See if I care! I like it like this. By the way, I've spoken to the Brummies. We have to get up tomorrow morning at eight o'clock. At nine they're coming round with the car to pick us up for the tour around the island.»

«D'ya know what, I've been thinking about that ...»

«I mighta guessed!» Brenda was drumming her fingertips against her temples again. «I s'pose you'd rather spend the day with your new lover?»

«How d'ya guess?»

«Now come on. Who d'ya think I am? I know queens! Are you in love then?»

«Well, a bit.»

«How long's 'e stayin' on the island?»

«Till Saturday.»

«Oh you poor thing. Then you've only got another three days.»

«What? But today's only Monday.»

«Sorry luvvey, today's Wednesday.»

Now I was really naffed off!

## Jacob's Favourite Camel,
## Or: Beware of Woolly Naffs!

«There's still time,» said Martin, and snapped shut the locks on his case. I looked at my watch. It was eight. He had to be at the airport by nine thirty. In the next room John, Martin's holiday companion, was rummaging around packing up his stuff. I closed the door, stretched out on the bed and crossed my arms behind my head. Martin took his winter jacket out of the cupboard and threw it over his suitcase.

«It's zero degrees and drizzle at Gatwick,» he said.

«How awful!» I watched him fold up his air ticket and stuff it into his back pocket.

«If the plane gets in on time I should be able to get a connection up to Coventry. It's been snowin' there.»

Martin suddenly pulled open a drawer, looked inside, and pushed it shut again. «I'm pretty sure I've got everything,» he said as his gaze travelled around the spartan room. Then he lay down next to me. I pulled my hands from behind my head and took him into my arms.

We'd spent the last, all too short, night together at my place in the *Europlaya Club*. Our trip had taken longer than we'd planned. The proliferous vegetation on the other side of the island had inspired us. We hiked through the wild landscape on the Roque Nublo, we saw the snow-capped peak of the Teide emerging from misty clouds in the distance.

The spicy scent of the pine forests had tempted us, and I picked two leaves from a tree in a bay leaf grove. In the afternoon we wandered through forests of spruce and palm trees and sat silently at the edge of the crater of the *Pico de Bandama*. Later our little Panda brought us over bumpy tracks through a maze of green valleys further to the north.

The sun was already quite low in the sky when we arrived at the Costa de Banaderos. Up high on a plateau overlooking the coast we stopped for a picnic of bread, cheese and red wine between gorse bushes. We looked out over the choppy sea and watched the surf breaking on the rocks below.

«Shall we head back?»

«Maybe there's somewhere here we could stay the night.»

And in the third village we found somewhere. The next morning we meandered through small settlements, stopped wherever the fancy took us, and had a look at some of the remains that the Spanish had left over from the Guanches. Then we headed back through Agaete and Mogán to Playa.

I felt Martin's breath on my skin, the warmth of his hand on my chest.

«It's been wonderful,» he said.

I repeated his words.

«Does our agreement still stand?»

«Yeah.»

John tapped on the door. «Would passengers to Gatwick please proceed to Gate Number 1.» We stood up and gave each other a big hug.

I picked up Martin's winter jacket and he carried the suitcase down to the street. In the taxi our hands found each other again, secretly, on the back seat, hidden from the driver's eyes.

«All the best.» I tried to smile, squeezed his hand, and stroked the back of his head one last time in farewell. He bent over towards me; our lips touched for a last second.

«It still stands ...»

I tapped the driver on the shoulder. «Would you please stop at the *Europlaya Club*.»

He braked sharply and I got out. Then, as the cab drove off Martin slid over onto the seat I had just vacated and poked his head out of the window. «It still stands ...»

I nodded and waved as long as I could still see his gorgeous head with his hair blowing in the wind.

That's how it was. And I really did only cry a wee little bit!

«Once again you look like a cross between a headmistress and a dressage rider, dear. Whassup?» said Brenda when I came in with a crusty loaf, a large box of cornflakes and some of them plastic bottles of water. First I had to have some decent breakfast to get my strength back.

«Don't give me that now! I'm a bit sensitive this mornin', I have to come to terms with a serious loss.»

«Oh, I see. Shall I put on the appropriate Carpenters' album?»

«Do you have to?»

«Some Beethoven perhaps?»

«Maybe.»

«I'll 'ave a look see what we've got.» Brenda went to the record cupboard and had a good rummage around.

«The Fifth?»

«Oh no, I couldn't be doin' with that now. Isn't the Sixth there?»

«I think so, but it's a bit scratched.»

After I'd recharged my emotional batteries with a bit of Beethoven, in spite of the scratches, I just wanted to go back to bed to catch up on some much-needed sleep and recharge my physical batteries.

«Oh, come on. You can do that at the beach,» said Brenda, «it'll stop you moping around here on your own all day.»

So I went along.

But although nothing at all had changed on the gay beach it all seemed quite different to me. Maybe it was because I hadn't slept much the last few nights or maybe because it was such a warm summery day. There was no cooling wind, and at midday hot heavy air hung over the scorched sand. I slept restlessly, dreamt from time to time, woke up to wipe the sweat from my brow and then fell back into a bizarre dream: It was the sun umbrellas that changed first. Their iron poles grew into mighty stone columns; the brightly coloured shades lost their colour and mutated above the columns into a dark roof that kept out all traces of sunlight. I felt as though I was locked in. Oil lamps gave out a restless, flickering light. Anxiously I looked around, I could make out people all around me who, like me, were sitting on the floor. There was a strange pungent odour. Nobody spoke, nobody moved, and yet I sensed a restless expectation.

Which darkroom have you landed up in this time? I asked myself, when suddenly a voice roared through the dimly lit hall like a clap of thunder.

«The Happy Hour of Copulation has come. Astarte, Her Mighty Highness, welcomes you to her Holy Temple. May the flames of love free you all!» announced the mighty voice.

«Oh God, oh Goddess!» I murmured, completely shocked, when I realised where I'd been transported to. «This is ancient Babylon! You're in the temple of Astarte, the Goddess of fertility. How on earth are you gonna get outta this stinkin' hole?» I wanted to get up, but some force held me down on the ground.

Suddenly there was movement. We all poked our heads up. Men, loads of men came into the hall, walked up and down the rows of people squatting on the ground, looked, rummaged around in the meagre light of the oil lamps, groped between legs, felt bodies in silence, and then turned away to begin again somewhere else. Some found what they were looking for and writhed around on the floor for a while in honour of Astarte. Then after the copulation was over I heard a metallic clank and saw both of them, the one who'd been squatting on the ground as well as the guard, get up and leave the temple together through a great gate.

But that didn't happen often. Most of them stayed where they were. In Astarte's temple.

«Everyone of you has his chance! The Hour of Copulation

121

is over!» thundered the hidden voice through the great room. Then it was quiet again. The gate closed in silence. We were all left behind in the temple. Next to me someone sighed and murmured quietly, as if to himself: «Maybe next time!»

«Hey, what on earth are you on about down there?» I suddenly heard Brenda's voice next to me.

I opened my eyes. The sun was bright.

«Who? Me?» I asked, dragged myself up from the sun lounger totally befuddled, and wiped the sweat from my brow. Then I looked around me. Everything was as it always had been.

«Well, who else? D'ya think I'm 'earin voices from t'other side or what? I'm not Doris Stokes you know! You'd better go and cool off in t'water. Or 'ave you got sunstroke already?»

I rummaged around in my beach bag looking for my watch. But I couldn't find it.

«What are you lookin' for then?»

«Me watch.»

«Oh these awful beach bags, they really are the bane of a woman's life,» Brenda cackled, «you can never find a bloody thing in them. Now my friend Dolly always says ...»

«Oh, there it is.» It was half past one. I'd been asleep for three hours. By now Martin was up in the air somewhere over southern Spain.

So then I decided to jump into the water and splash about for half an hour. That's always good for raising your spirits. Not just coz the water's so refreshing, but also coz you have to be so careful that the waves don't knock you for six.

«Ven ze vaves are zo ztrong I cannot conzentrate on ze beautiful men,» complained Heidi. «As zoon az I haff found a nize vun I haff ze stomach full ov salty vater!»

«Then maybe you should try keeping your mouth shut.»

«Ach, I alvays forget it,» she said, and from then on she just didn't go into the water if the waves were too strong. But that was exactly what I liked so much. And so did the Bald Baritone.

Now she was a very nice opera singer from somewhere in the Midlands. And coz he hardly had any hair on his head that's what we called him.

Anyway, I often bumped into the Bald Baritone in the water. She had this incredible way of riding on the waves. Not with a surfboard but just on her hands and feet.

«How on earth do you do that?» I asked her.

«Oh, it's really easy. As soon as a good wave breaks you just fling yourself in front of it like some suicidal queen in front of a No. 7 bus. Then stretch out and let the wave wash you onto the shore. And you have to steer a bit with you hands.»

«And what about your feet?»

«You have to waggle them a bit, as if you had flippers on.»

So that's exactly what I tried to do. But sometimes the wave wasn't right, and sometimes I forgot that bit with the feet and somehow I just couldn't get the hang of it at all. In the end I was covered in scratches all over my stomach where the waves had dragged me over the beach.

«Hey, what's with all these somersaults? You've been at it all day?» asked Vera when she saw me practising.

«Come on, why don't you give it a try too. The Bald Baritone says it's all just a question of practice. So I explained it to Vera and we practised body surfing together for a while. But she couldn't get the hang of it either.

«Oh, this is all too much for a white woman!» she said after a while. «I'm gettin' out.»

«I'll come by in a minute. Where are you posted today?»

«Right in the front of the paupers' section.» That's what Vera called the part of the beach just to the left of the gay section.

If there wasn't any wind you could spread yourself out really nicely in the sand there without having to rent one of them dreadfully overpriced sun loungers. We lay there sometimes as well. But never in those awful stony sandcastles a bit further up. Usually there's some couple or other squatting in them –

123

like brooding chickens with their necks stretched up just far enough for them to peek over the stone wall.

That's where I stumbled across Miss Chase with her boy-friend. She was a French specimen from the Lorraine region; hence Miss Chase! To begin with I actually thought she was quite nice. But after a while I realised she was only being nice to me coz they were after a threesome. And as soon as they caught on that I wasn't interested they came over all bitchy. Now I mean I've nothing against threesomes, in principle at least. But surely you have to be at least a bit physically compatible before you get involved in that sort of stuff, don't you? Now some people really go so sex-mad on their hols. If they don't get just what they want straight away they turn into complete bitches from hell!

Anyway, when I went to visit Vera in the slums she was just putting a beauty magazine aside and said, «Listen, are you gonna be at home around Easter?»

«I dunno yet, why?»

«Well, in the week before Easter I'm gonna be in the Prince Hotel in Greenwich. I thought maybe I'd come an' see you.»

«Best give us a ring first. Whatya doin' in Greenwich?»

«A beauty seminar. *Beauty through Bees* it's called.»

«You don't 'ave to get stung for that full-lipped look, do you?»

«Nah, I don't think so. They do all beauty products with bee things. It's just kinder to the skin, that's all. Better than all that chemical shit all the time.»

«Yeah, a real beeswax mask works wonders for your face don't it?»

«Exactly. I always have such terrible problems with my skin anyway. Not long now and I'll 'ave to seriously think about gettin' a face-lift.»

«Not yet surely?»

«Look. Around my eyes it's already startin' to wrinkle!» Vera pulled the skin under her eyes taut to show me the difference.

«Now you look like one of them geisha girls.»

«That don't matter. That'd go better with my feet then.»

«How come?»

«For my size they're far too small.»

Now I'd never noticed that before. Usually girls are quite happy when they don't have such great big tootsies. But Vera wanted bigger ones.

Well we all have our little problem zones don't we? Now me for example, I'd really like to have a little more padding around the bum. It really could do with being a bit rounder. «Isn't there anything I can do?» I asked Vera, coz she really is the expert on all matters cosmetic. You see she has this fabulous girlfriend who works in a beauty salon. She gets all her tips from her.

«Maybe you could get yerself some silicon injections. That'd give you some padding at least.»

«Oh, I dunno though. It might look OK when you're standing up, but when you're sittin' down, wouldn't it feel like you were perchin' on the edge of a water bed?»

And just as we were chit-chattin' away about our minor defects, along came Cinder-Ella. Now she's this girl from Norwich. Her real name is Ben but she runs a funeral parlour and specialises in cremation. So that's why we called her Cinder-Ella. She looked completely dishevelled and somehow rather ravished rather than ravishing.

«You've not been pillaged by a gang of Vikings have you?»

«No, I wouldn't exactly say that,» panted Cinder-Ella, and gasped for breath. «It was the temptation of the Devil himself that lured me.»

«Oh, you've been up Bongoland, haven't you, dirty bitch!»

«Not at all,» she puffed. «Sorry, I 'ave to catch my breath first.»

«I'm sure the Red Cross has got some portable breathing apparatus here somewhere. Shall I see what I can rustle up?»

«No, leave it. It was just fantastic.»

«Well, what then?»

«Well, I was just wanderin' about at the edge of the dunes over there. And as I looked more closely at that sandcastle I saw these two blokes lookin' out. I dunno, I s'pose I must've got a bit too close or summink, coz all of a sudden I was in there wiv'em. It was fantastic.»

«How brave, she knocked off two Viking warriors in one go!»

«No they were French. Oh, those French boys' bodies, I could worship them all day!» beamed Cinder-Ella quite happy and contented, and wandered back off to her sun lounger to have a lie down.

«Mmhhh,» sighed Vera. «You know, Priscilla Presley was quite right when she said: *A single moment can change your life.*»

«You know, when Cinder-Ella starts worshippin' bodies you'd better hide your matches!» I said. And so another day on the beach came to an end.

I was starting to feel like the Milky Bar kid. I mean, over the weeks I had got quite brown. But not like Vera. She was almost black from head to toe. But unfortunately she and her gang left the next day.

It wasn't long before Brenda and me were the only ones left from our bunch. The Queen Bee, Alessandro, Lucy in the Sky and the Brummies all shot off home that weekend as well.

They always seem to come and go in waves in Playa. Internationally speaking as well. Over Christmas and New Year the clientele is generally quite chic. But after New Year that really changes. Particularly once the dog-loving fraternity arrive by the coachload. You honestly can't believe all the yapping and burrowing that goes on down the beach once that lot show up.

Queens and their pooches, that's a book all by itself. I must say I didn't notice if the naffs in Playa were dragging any sorts of creatures around with them, apart from their sprogs. But that's probably coz we didn't take much notice of the naffs anyway.

At any rate, after the second week of January there were about two and a half pooches to every four queens, statistically speaking. Funnily enough they always seemed to congregate in the first row at the gay beach.

«Have you noticed how these mutts always seem to look like their mistresses?» Brenda observed. She wasn't a happy camper. Each time she got a load of sand in her face or on the book she was reading she almost had a heart attack.

«These bloody mongrels are really startin' to get on my tits!» she moaned, and shook the sand off again. Just across from her this little rat was burrowing away in the ground and kept kicking up sand in a wide arc behind it, and the accompanying yapping was most annoying.

«D'ya think its mistress'll start diggin' too?» I was about to ask, when all of a sudden there was a shrill, high-pitched scream and the mistress toppled backwards, sun lounger and all, right into the hole her very own doggy had been digging.

«Serves 'er right! I hope they both get stuck down there forever,» muttered Brenda spitefully.

But only the little rat had disappeared. Completely gone, buried under a ton of sand and its mistress. At first the wretched little thing let out a pitiful short yelp and then ... silence.

«Thank heavens for that,» I was just thinking, when suddenly the mistress started carrying on like nobody's business: «Princess! Princess!» she shrieked, and started burrowing away at the ground.

«You're quite right, you know,» I said to Brenda, «the likeness is truly remarkable!»

She started burrowin' away in the sand with her hands like a woman possessed, and after a while she managed to grab hold of the stupid mutt. Naturally it was a poodle!

But after she'd succeeded in shaking off most of the sand, accompanied by cries of «Princess, Princess, speak to me!», the wretched thing still looked pretty yellow.

«Champagne poodles are totally out,» mumbled Brenda. «She should've left the bloody thing down that 'ole!»

«Maybe you can get'em dyed.»

«Never mind dyed, I'd be quite happy wi' dead! Though I've heard the punk look's quite the rage for poodles these days. Or even violet with sandy stripes might come quite nice.»

«I couldn't really care about the colour as long as the damned things don't yap all day and shit all over the place.»

The worst one for that was Juliet! A poodle as well of course, but a black one this time, done up like a Persian. I think someone must've bitten off its tail or something coz all it had was a little black stump, which it waggled around nervously like it had a loose connection in its arse! Now of course, every one of these mongrels had its own distinctive personal bark. But this particular specimen had such a nerve-shredding, wailing, whimpering pitch that you really couldn't help seriously wanting to drown it! And at least once a day it had a fit. Then the hateful thing made such a racket you just had to stick your fingers in you ears.

«Rat poison, rat poison,» chimed a chorus from the loungers behind us. But nobody actually got around to fetching some. And this was another prime example of how some people and their doggies are just so alike. You see, when Juliet's mistress started yapping you could hear her all the way up the beach, whether you wanted to or not.

But there was one good-natured pooch that came down to the beach. It was a great black bristly creature that would lie contentedly under a sun lounger and sometimes even went swimming with its mistress. Yes, it was really salt-waterproof.

And even in *Café Wien* it was quite happy lying under the table and not sitting up at it like all the spoilt poodles.

In my opinion, that's really the thing with some queens and their doggies. They can't have kids so they go and get themselves something like that instead. It's not great, but it's better than falling in love with a camel!

«Well, I'd better be off, I've got to go and buy more greens,» said Joe, and ran off up the beach. He was from Stoke-on-Trent, was here on his own, and was totally loopy about animals.

I mean, some queers have queer eating habits but it didn't take long even for me to work out that no one gets through several whole bags of greens every day.

«What are you doin' with all them greens?» I asked one day.

«It's for Fatima.»

«Who's that then?»

«My favourite camel o' course!» he said, and looked at me as if I had a screw loose.

«Oh, I see,» I said, somewhat bemused.

But once I stopped to consider where and how someone from Stoke-on-Trent could keep a camel in Playa, I did start to get a bit curious.

«How big is this Fatima then?» I asked.

Again he looked at me as if I wasn't quite right in the head. «'Aven't you ever seen a camel or what?»

«D'ya keep Fatima on the balcony then?»

«Don't be silly! She is locked up though.»

«What, in the apartment?»

«No, in the caravansary.»

«Oh, I see,» I murmured very carefully. But then I remembered there was always this bunch of camels you could see from the bus that runs from Maspalomas to Playa. Joe had gone to see this caravansary, and ever since then he ran out there every day with bags full of leaves.

«Yes, I fell in love with Fatima the second I set eyes on her.

She's so nice. So gentle and trusting. Just lovely. Have you ever felt camel lips on you skin?»

«Urgh! No!»

«D'ya fancy comin' along one day?»

«Well, I dunno ... we've only got a couple more days, and then ...»

«I'm tellin' you, they're real soft, right gentle.»

I mean really! What on earth can you say to that? You know, I think there really isn't enough love between people these days.

«You know what?» Brenda said to me when I came home. «All these weeks we've been in Playa we've only hung around with queens. We should try and get used to naffs again.»

«D'ya think so?»

«Yeah, only this afternoon Harry from Milton-Keynes was saying that after every Playa holiday it's real hard work getting used to naff-speak again. We could get started on it now.»

«How d'ya mean? We don't live in Milton-Keynes!»

«Well, in a sense there's a bitta Milton-Keynes everywhere ain't there?» said Brenda, and started flicking through one of those bright leaflets that always get shoved through the door.

«Should we plonk ourselves down in between all them breeders on the beach then, or what?»

«We needn't go that far!»

«Or we could go to *La Belle*?» That's this naff bar in the *Yumbo* where a very clever pair of queens give the naffs a basic course in camping it up.

«No, nothing like that!» said Brenda, luckily dismissing such hellish prospects. «We could go on one o' these strawberry picking trips the naffs do.»

«You mean like them trips to Calais to get cheap beer, but in Spanish? Do we really 'ave to?»

«Yes,» said Brenda, «let's do one. You'd get loadsa prezzies.»

«What, from you?»

«No stupid, from the naffs o' course. Look at this 'ere.»

She shoved a handful of leaflets into my face, with great big bright slogans on them. «Read this!»

*The New Strawberry Trip:*
*Gran Canaria's most beautiful tours, just like in the movies. Free with every booking: 1 punnet of fresh strawberries, real English breakfast, 1 bottle of Spanish wine, a video souvenir of the island (1 per couple). Travel in modern, air-conditioned coaches.*

«D'ya think the naffs'd count us as a couple?»

«If you really want the video you'll 'ave to drag up! We could do a Guanche tour instead though, or the caves and almond blossom tour, or a trip to the festival of the caves.»

*Free invitation to a once-in-a-lifttime experience: the festival of the caves,* I read on. *No advertising for wool blankets!* «What's this about advertising for wool blankets?»

«Ignore that one. Only death's for free. You 'ave to put up with a bitta advertising. Let's do the tour of the Canarian villages. You get free tablecloths on that'n.»

In the end we plumped for the tour of the villages. But only coz Brenda'd got this bee in her bonnet about spending more time with breeders!

So, three days before the end of our holiday there we were at nine o'clock in the morning waiting outside the hotel *Don Miguel.* That's where we were supposed to get picked up, you see, and there were already hordes of naffs hanging about. Now over the years you really do develop a knack for telling who's gay and who isn't, and I'm telling you there wasn't one single queen amongst them. Now that really should've been a warning!

And there was no sign of the village tour whatsoever, although every few minutes some coach or other came thundering by for fruit, bush or tropical tours. At ten we were still standing there.

«Well, naffs are naffs if you ask me!» I said to Brenda. «It don't really make any difference what bus we get on!»

«OK then, we'll just take the next bus that comes along.»

Now this happened to be a tour called *Gran Canaria! Olé!*

«All aboard,» called out this rather glamorous straight number. «We do the village tour too.»

So I tottered on behind Brenda and was just about to sit down next to her when this very determined fat naff in a straw hat shoved its way past me and plonked itself down on the seat next to her. I was most unimpressed. So I had to sit behind them on my own.

The breeder started yakking away before we'd even set off, and was into a right old interrogation routine before we'd reached the end of the street. Where was Brenda staying, where did she come from, how long was she there for, whether she was on holiday alone. «Oh, you're not married then?»

«No.»

«But you're such a nice-looking young man! Oh well, I suppose good old-fashioned marriage is falling more and more out of fashion.»

«I s'pose so,» was Brenda's uncharacteristically brief answer. Then at least she shut up for a bit.

«Of course some men just take off their wedding rings when they're on holiday don't they?», and then she laughed flirtatiously.

Brenda didn't say a word.

«My ex-husband and me went on holiday on our own in the end as well. I mean, sometimes it's a good thing if you can enjoy your own space isn't it?» I heard her saying. «I expect your girlfriend can't wait to see you after your holiday, can she?»

What did she mean 'can't wait to see you'? She's sitting right behind you! I thought, and then said out loud: «I say Brendan, why don't you get a cactus to take back for Elvira. I see they're very cheap here.» They were too. The bus had just stopped out-side a supermarket to pick up more people.

«Oh, is that your girlfriend's name, Elvira?» said the fat bree-der, smiling at me. Apparently she had just realised that Brenda and I knew one another.

«Yes, and she collects cacti,» I explained.

«That's a lovely hobby,» she said, and bang! I was lumbered with her too. But I just kept talking really queeny through my nose at her and she gradually lost interest. I had absolutely no intention whatsoever of sitting there all on my tod, letting this pushy old tart monopolise Brenda for the whole trip. She was obviously just after a bloke to give her one!

But finally we managed to get rid of her. A couple of miles further down the road we had to change onto another coach at this big bus station where they sorted out all the tourists into groups for the various trips. We waited over an hour till the coach set off.

«Good morning. I'm Terry, your tour guide for today,» this chap suddenly called out. «*The Gran Canaria! Olé!* tour has had to be cancelled I'm afraid. We're gonna be doing the combined caves and almond blossom tour. Of course you'll still all get the presents from the *Olé!* tour after lunch.»

By this time I was already starving though, coz it was nearly twelve.

«When is lunch?» asked a grey-haired pair of pensioners from Bognor Regis in front of us.

«After the advertising presentation, ladies and gentlemen,» said Terry. «Our company is delighted to be able to present to you the new collection of luxury *Llama Diamond* Pure Wool Blankets. But both before and after you'll experience the unique landscape of this heavenly island on a dream tour. Who hasn't already dreamt of enjoying the enchanting lure of this delight-ful countryside under the blossoms of an almond tree?»

«Oh shit!» I said, «wool blankets after all.»

«You only get saucepans on the Guanche tour,» said the pensioner in front of us.

«Oh, what a shame,» said Brenda.

«Yes, but on this trip you get a watch,» said the OAP. «We do one of these tours every other day. My husband can't walk so well anymore you see, and at least he gets to see some of the island like this.»

After half an hour we had to get off the coach and were shepherded onto a camel farm. Now it wasn't as if they were giving the camels away for nothing, oh no! They wanted a thousand pesetas for a camel ride.

«They're not taking me for a ride» said Brenda, and flatly refused to set foot – or anything else – on the camels.

«But look, loads o' the naffs are doin' it. And you're not joinin' in again.»

«That's not what I meant,» she said real stroppy, and treated herself to a cup of coffee in the camel stables instead.

Then later, the coach stopped at this pub where they wanted us to try this sticky banana liquor stuff (and buy it of course) and some nibbles. We didn't mind that though coz we were starving hungry by then.

At about half past twelve, I was well narked by this time, coz the naffs had all started singing *You take the low road and I'll take the high road,* and coz it was getting steeper and steeper and more and more bendy the tour guide handed out sick bags. But just my luck, not a single naff threw up. Although Brenda did look a bit green every now and then.

«Why don't you try singin' along a bit,» I said, «it might help.»

She wasn't having any of that though, and just stuck her fingers in her ears and stared bad-temperedly into her sick bag. And so we made our way to San Bartolome.

«You'll receive your lunch vouchers after the advertising presentation,» announced the tour guide after we'd all been bustled up to the first floor of this building. There were white garden chairs and tables all around, and up on a podium were various beds with wool blankets over them.

«Ladies and gentlemen, please help yourselves to a small snack, courtesy of our company. And if the gentlemen would be so kind as to serve the ladies,» announced the naff receptionist, who as it turned out was a blanket expert too. The small snack consisted of McVitie's biscuits and lemonade, and of course I was so starving I dived straight into them.

«Well, I must say you're a very rude gentleman. Why aren't you servin' me then?» Brenda snapped.

«Oh, I'm so sorry. You usually manage all right on your own!» So I took some biscuits from the platter, placed them delicately one at a time into Brenda's hand, and she nibbled them like a proper lady.

And then the wool blanket performance started. Two whole hours of it!

Now I don't know if you're one of those filthy beasts that sleeps under feather or down quilts. You might as well sleep in the dustbin! Apparently we Brits are particularly dirty pigs in this regard. About fifty per cent of us have a rubbish dump in our beds, and you wouldn't believe what goes on in there. The bed bugs do the cha-cha in it. All night long! In the first year when the feathers are quite new there are only about a million or so of them dancing around. But after five years there's about 25 to 30 million leaping about ... At least that's what this blanket expert naffess would have us believe.

«Can you imagine what a racket they must make? Now you know why you always have so much trouble gettin' to sleep,» I said to Brenda.

«D'ya think so? Actually I quite like the cha-cha.»

«Yeah, but when millions of bugs are dancin' it in your bed it can't be all that pleasant.»

«No,» said the blanket expert naffess, «of course it's not plea-

135

sant. The bugs lay at least half a million eggs every day. And, ladies and gentlemen, they incubate these eggs every night. And then, don't forget, they have to go to the loo don't they? Now is there a loo in your bed? Of course not. So where do they do their doings? In your bed of course. Your bed is full of dried bed bug poop! Your feather quilt is quite simply a dung heap!»

«Oh my Gawdd! I didn't know that!» wailed Brenda. «I have to have one of them wool blankets. I won't spend another night in that bed bug shit heap!»

«Now don't let the naffs get you all worked up,» I tried to calm her down.

«And now, ladies and gentlemen, I'll show you what a bed bug actually looks like,» said the naffess. She dimmed the lights and switched on a slide projector.

Not just Brenda but the whole hall let out a cry of disgust.

«That's terrible!»

«Oh, I can't stand it!»

«Disgusting!»

«For heaven's sake, how much are the wool blankets?» shouted a particularly disturbed old person across the room.

«Well, I can make you several fantastic offers. Here we have the Rolls Royce of wool blankets. It costs just £ 599 plus postage and packing. Over here we have the merino lamb blanket, virgin wool from the slopes of the Himalayas for £ 399. And this one here is the fabulous lama alpaca creation also for £ 399. And next to that the top-quality mohair blanket for the sensational price of only £ 299!» Loads of naffs suddenly stormed up to the stage and started rummaging through the blankets.

«I bet Terry Wogan's slept in all of them,» I said, as I sensed Brenda was about to rush off to join them.

«Rather him than all those shitty bug monsters!» she said, and shot off to the podium.

For a whole hour the blanket expert naffess kept on and on

at the hapless tourists and even managed to persuade some of them to buy.

Brenda though stood quite undecided between the Rolls Royce and the Himalaya blankets. «I just can't decide. Both of them are so fabulous aren't they? Or should I get the Rolls Royce?»

«Come and have another glass of lemonade!» I said, and with that I managed to tempt her back over to the table. «Let's think it over carefully.» But I only managed to talk her out of buying one coz she was so awfully hungry by now too.

«Yes, you're right,» she said in the end. «You shouldn't really make big decisions on an empty stomach.» But the blanket-naffs were not prepared to give up that easily. They just kept rabbiting on and on. They had no scruples! The bus that was supposed to come and pick us up simply didn't come.

«Well, I'm gonna call Amnesty International,» I said. «I'm being held prisoner and tortured by naffs!»

«What do you mean, tortured?»

«Mental torture, food deprivation and brainwashing! They're just gonna let us starve till we sign a contract!»

«Well I'm not signin' anything!»

«Then you'll starve. These blanket naffs are as hard as nails!» But then we did manage to get out after all coz the pensioner woman from Bognor Regis had a total fit.

«When am I gonna get my watch?!!» she screamed, grabbed her husband's walking stick, and started bangin' on all the tables with it makin' a right din. «I want my tablecloth and the video! You promised it me last time and I haven't had a thing!»

And when the others started asking about their bottles of wine, the crocodile farm, the parrot show and the caves, the blanket naffs were forced onto the defensive. Then we threatened them with Amnesty International and at last the coach came. We were on the road for a whole hour until we finally got to the crocodile farm where we were supposed to get something to eat. By this time it was about five. But first we had to form a queue, get counted, and then we had to wait again. As we were standing around waiting, these frightful animal noises came from somewhere in the farm.

«What on earth are those terrible screams?»

«Probably a crocodile that's just gettin' made into a handbag!» said Brenda.

«Oh, d'ya think we'll get a crocky bag?»

«If it's edible I'll certainly 'ave it!»

Then, completely starving, we were herded into an enormous beer tent. At least two hundred naffs were squatting on long wooden benches and gobbling down mountains of Smash and incredibly thin slices of beef and gravy. For dessert there was a parrot show! The compere pretended to be a bullfighter and the parrot was the bull, and all the naffs kept yelling *olé!*

«The passengers from bus number seventy four can collect their gifts now,» announced Terry, the tour guide. «But please hurry up because the crocodile show is about to begin.»

I shot off straight away coz I at least wanted to get the bottle of wine to drown my sorrows.

At the gift kiosk between all the crocodile pools, I bumped into the OAP from Bognor Regis again. She was furious.

«They've only got tablecloths,» she said in a rage.

«What, no wine?»

«No, and no watches and no videos either! They're supposed to be coming tomorrow. So I'll be comin' again. And now I'm off to the crocodile show. At least that's something we don't get to see every day in Bognor.»

When I got back to Brenda she looked like she'd been kissed by an alligator. «All of this is really gettin' on my tits!» she complained.

«'Ave you had enough of the naffs, or what?»

«I wanna go home!»

I wanted to as well. But we couldn't, coz we all got dragged off again. This time to the cave-men. We had to go an' see them, coz obviously the tour guide wanted to cash in on the commission he got from them. For the wine and the cheese that got sold to the *Olé*-naffs there.

It was pitch-dark by the time we got back to Playa and finally escaped the clutches of the blanket naffs.

«Never again!» swore Brenda. «I'd rather share my bed with them bugs than spend another minute wi' them woolly naffs!»

«You were the one who wanted to get used to them again.»

«Oh, you really musta misunderstood me there!»

«Well let's celebrate anyway. Why don't you cook something fabulous?»

So she did. I went out and got a lovely bottle of wine and a delicious tub of ice cream. And later, as we were sitting down with our coffee and brandy, we put the Carpenters on and began to really enjoy our freedom again. I gradually became myself again and got over my naff-trauma.

*Rainy days and Mondays always get me down.*

«You know what?» Brenda suddenly asked.

«What?»

«We should go to *Centre Stage* tomorrow evening, it's just sooo much fun.» And so that's what we did. It's a real cosy little shoe box in *Yumbo* with a couple of queens behind the bar who really get everyone going. They pass around tambourines and hats and wigs and all sorts of outrageous drag and show clips from musicals and stuff on a big TV and get everyone to sing along and act out scenes from the shows.

The walls are all full of posters and photos of all the stars we love. And even the music is selected especially for the international gay community. If Judy Garland wasn't singing *Somewhere Over the Rainbow* then it was Marlene Dietrich for the German patrons and then Liza Minnelli or Babs or Shirley Bassey and even occasionally Lola Flores or Isabel Pantosa for the Spanish.

«This is pure occupational therapy,» said Brenda, and

banged about clumsily on a tambourine. «Don't you think lotsa these girls somehow look the same?»

And just as I was saying that, the old Liza classic from *Caba-ret* started up, *Farewell mein lieber Herr* ...

That really got the girls going!

At least half of them started bobbing' about on their stools doing Liza routines. Whether they were London Lillies, Berlin Betties or Madrid Manuelas they all sang along to the words. With a bitta drag around their necks or on their heads they were in their element. And some of them even looked like they might really have been related to Ms. Minnelli!

«D'ya think this is their way of dealin' with traumatic experiences, or what?» asked Brenda.

«Yeah, maybe it is. Maybe they've just been around naffs for too long!»

«Exactly!» piped up a voice beside me all of a sudden, and stopped singing along with Liza. «We've met before. You were sitting in front of me on the plane.»

It was Geoffrey! He'd combed his hair just like Liza, was wearing a bright feather boa around his neck, and was completely off his tits!

«Yes, today is Liza Minnelli evening,» he announced with a beaming smile.

«Is your mother here as Liza an' all?» Brenda asked her.

«No, I'm just in the process of getting over her.»

«How are you doin' that then?»

«She's back home in Romford now and is mad as hell at me. But I don't care. I'm gonna get me own place, once and for all! I mean, at 35 you shouldn't be livin' with your mother anyway.»

«And what about Cynthia? What're you gonna do with her?».

«Mother just took her with her. She's tryin' to blackmail me with her! She knows damned well I'm very attached to the little angel. That's why she stole her from me. But let her! I'm

140

burnin' my bridges. I phoned work today and arranged to take me whole year's holiday in one go. I'm stayin' another three weeks.»

«Now that's quite a turn-up for the books, innit?» said Brenda.

«Yes, I've finally found the man of my dreams, Julio. He lives here on the island in Arucas and we love each other and he's gonna come back with me to England and we're gonna live together.»

«Wow, how romantic ...!» sighed Brenda.

«I imagine your mother feels totally left out of your life now,» I said.

«Tough tits! She's always known I'm gay but she would never talk about it. So serves 'er right!» Well I never! The adventures some girls get themselves into!

«When are you leavin'?» Geoffrey suddenly asked us, and straightened up his drag.

«The day after tomorrow.»

«Could you take back a letter for my mother? The post always takes forever from here.»

«You could always phone 'er if it's urgent,» said Brenda, practical as ever in a crisis.

«It's not urgent. But important, and some things are better written than said.»

So the next evening Geoffrey brought round a great fat letter for mummy, and we jetted off home with this dramatic dispatch in our saddle bags.

«I hope the old girl doesn't 'ave a heart attack when she reads it,» said Brenda once we were on the plane.

«I'm sure Geoffrey'll 'ave written it all very diplomatic.»

«Why d'ya think that?»

«I know *gays and their mothers!* They sulk for a bit, but they always patch things up in the end.»

«Now I really do think you're oversimplifying again ...»

And believe it or not, there we were sitting on the plane on the way home and were once again deeply involved in the never-ending topic of *gays and their mothers*.

And so it was that our crazy Gran Canaria holiday drew to a close. We'd got a gorgeous tan, had a lovely rest, had loads of fun, and had sworn to return very soon to Playa del Ingles. Just for the hell of it!

Maybe we'll see you there.

Bye.

## *Folk dancing in the Yumbo Centre*
### *Or: The Dance of the Washerwomen*

Well, of course the next year I was straight back to Playa for my Christmas hols, but unfortunately this time without my very very bestest girlfriend in the whole wide world.

«No,» said Brenda, «I wanna go to Florida. I mean the sun shines there an' all and they've got gay beaches two to the dozen!»

«What 'ave you got against Playa all of a sudden? Didn't you enjoy yerself last year then?» I asked her.

«Of course I did. But I've always wanted to go to Florida. And this year I'm just gonna, that's all!»

And so it was. There was no talkin' to 'er. When she gets a bee in her bonnet that's it. And she'd certainly got her heart set on Florida. Personally I think it was one of those naughty films about surfing boys that sowed that seed, but enough said about that dirty little habit!

In the end though Brenda didn't get anywhere near Key West but spent three weeks squattin' on the neighbouring island to Gran Canaria, La Palma, in the pouring rain!

At first you see she tried to coax her girlfriend Angie to go with her to Florida, but after a disturbing number of tourists started disappearing there Angie wasn't having it. Apparently she had a complete fit and told Brenda to stuff her surfers where the sun don't shine – I imagine she meant Preston! She wanted to go somewhere with a bit of sunshine and where she had more than a fifty per cent chance of getting home alive. And so that's how they ended up on La Palma, last minute.

Vera, the Queen Bee, Alessandro and I all hoped Brenda would come and visit us between Christmas and New Year, but no! She stuck to her guns and sat there in the rain on La Palma the whole holiday. Now I know what she was going through, I spent a very long fortnight in Rhodes in the rain once, and that was more than enough for me. At any rate, in the four weeks that we were in Playa it only rained once.

Now Vera and me are the same – we can easily cope with more than two weeks in Playa, and so we booked a flight in the last cheap week before Christmas. You see, when you fly to Playa you have to take account of the fact that the flights get more and more expensive each week in the build-up to Christmas. And every year just before the Virgin Mary drops the sprog they cost almost double the usual price. Funny that, innit?!

«I'm not havin' that!» Vera and I said to each other. And so she flew out on the 8th December and I shot off after her the very next day. For four whole weeks! We stayed at the *Lenamar* – me on the fifth floor and Vera on the fourth on the other side – so I could always get a good look into her apartment. In the evenings we met up in *Nestor's*.

«What's it like this year then?» I asked her straight away.

«Well, the same as always, really!» she replied. «Just that the *Yumbo Centre* has got even gayer. Now they've got twenty-three gay bars, restaurants, shops and stuff like that.»

«So it's more convenient than ever, then? No more silly running backwards and forwards to the *Nilo*, thank God!»

«Exactly. *King's-Club* is now over here in the *Yumbo*. And if you need poppers or designer drawers or an outrageous swimming dress you can get all of that on t'way over. And you get a lovely placky bag to show off with at home. And where the old *Spartacus* was, there's a new German gay bar and the new *Spartacus* is just behind *Hummel-Hummel*, and then further on there's this German bar *Na Und*, and upstairs on the balcony *Tubos* has had a massive extension built and behind *Mykonos* there's *Why Not*, and then in the corner in front of *Metropol* there's *Claxx*, and we absolutely have to be there by three o'clock in the morning coz that's when the washerwomen'll be goin' crazy!»

«You're mad! Who in the world pegs out at three o'clock in the mornin'?»

«You'll see,» said Vera, and sipped at her Carrajillo. That's a kind of espresso with brandy in it. It comes lovely just after dinner, I can tellya.

And as I was sittin' there a-sippin' and a-slurpin' I had a good shufty round the place to see if there was anyone about I knew from the year before, when suddenly Vera gave me a sharp poke and said: «Look who's comin.'»

Well I never! It was Kenneth and Hakon, the two policemen from Sweden. Just like last year.

«No, what a coincidence. You're 'ere too!» I called out, and practically knocked them over with a big hug. Only in Playa could you get away with something like that! Back home the pigs tend to be so stand-offish, as if they're afraid of catching foot and mouth or something if you're just a little bit nice to 'em!

Anyway, we were still right in the thick of our hellos when all of a sudden from somewhere someone called out «Cooey!» And as I looked around to see who it was I clapped eyes on Ernie and Andrew, the Scottish OAPs from Sweden that I'd got to know and love the year before. They're Kenneth and Hakon's adopted parents, and they were sitting with their backs to us a couple of tables away so I hadn't noticed them in all the turmoil. So we picked up our things and went over to join them and celebrate our reunion.

«Aye well, if you come to Playa in December every year you're bound to bump into the same people now, aren't you dolly?» said Ernie, and waved to a friend from Sweden.

«But every now 'n' again some fresh meat gets flown in too,» whispered Vera, gave me a nudge, and pointed to two exceptionally good-looking young numbers headed toward our table. One of them was tall and slim with short black hair and the cutest smile you could possibly imagine. The other one was a bit smaller with blond hair and had a fabulous gym-trained body. They stopped right in front of our table and looked all around, obviously looking for someone.

«Oh, there you are,» called Kenneth.

«Now the whole family's together at last,» said Hakon.

«Och, this is Chris and Ralf, our adopted grandchildren,» Ernie explained to us, clearly the proud grandmother. «They're from Bath, an' me daughter Kenneth met 'em 'ere the yeer before last.»

Then they joined us as well. Although our table was overfull, I must say it was really sweet to see all three generations of the family together. I mean, it really is pretty rare for gay men of different generations to even have anything to say to each other, let alone get on so well and even go on holiday together.

«At my age, o' course, the child-bearing yeers are well and truly behind me,» said Ernie somewhat wistfully. «So I think it's fabulous when Hakon and Kenneth see to it that their friends become our friends too. Andrew and I feel so much more a part o' things then.»

«And in the summer we'll all meet up again as bridesmaids at the registry office in Stockholm,» said Chris.

«What d'ya mean?» asked Vera slightly confused.

«Well, in t'summer Ernie and me's gettin' married petal,» said Andrew. «In June that law's finally comin' out that means after 40 years we can at last stop livin' in sin! Maybe then we'll be the oldest married gay couple in Sweden, eh?»

But typically for the girls it wasn't long before they were bickering about the details.

«Well I'm throwin' the rice,» shouted Hakon.

«You'll 'ave to cook it first,» Kenneth called back.

«I might as well just sling them little plastic bags at 'em then!»

«Hey, why don't you two get married at the same time too?»

I asked Kenneth. «A double wedding, they're all the rage these days.»

«Oh I dunno. We're really not ready for that yet. We've only been livin' together for ten years. But I wouldn't say it's totally outta the question.»

So we chit-chatted a while about the latest fashions in brides' dresses and wedding menus and such till Vera suddenly said: «You know it's a bit odd. Usually at this time o' the year the hoof hammerer's gallopin' around all o'er the place. I ain't seen 'er at all yet this year. Three months ago she told me she'd be comin' out here again.»

«Oh, are you still in touch with her then?»

«Yeah, she calls me up two or three times a year from various hot spots. One year she was in Turkey building rockets for NATO or something, then she was in Paris making gold cock-rings for Cartier. And the last time I heard from her she was on some oilrig off the coast of Norway. Maybe she decided to stay there.»

«Oh, I doubt that. Spanish immigration probably refused to let her into Gran Canaria. She duffed up too many naffs last time!»

At half past twelve we set off for a crawl through the scene and tottered off to *Eden* first. The drag show was just getting underway.

«Oh, do we really have to?» I asked Vera, somewhat undecided. «These endless bloody drag shows ... I mean ... I really don't know.»

«Maybe the Spanish girls'll throw in a bit of folk dancing. At least then we'd get a bit more of a taste of the country and the people, eh?»

So, we went into *Eden*. At least it all sounded like authentic Spanish music. Once we'd managed to worm our way through the thick of it we saw this Spanish señora thrashing about on the stage. She had on this strange red dress that was much shorter at the front than at the back. You see, on the back she had this red 'n' white frilly extension built on what she kept swingin' backwards and forwards with one hand like she really couldn't stick red 'n' white skirt extensions! And with the other hand she flung open this glittering fan and waved it about in front of her face like she was having an attack of Parkinson's or something.

Every now and again, when the music and the singing got really dramatic, she would slap the fan shut, fling the array of skirts as far as they'd go, wave her arms in the air, and then thrust her hands onto her hips and start stamping about in a rage as if she was trying to kill a swarm of cockroaches. And perhaps coz she didn't manage this straight away she'd throw a nervous glance up into the air and stare for a second at the carnival garlands that were strung up left and right above the stage. The stamping dance, the turgid singing, and the bombastic music all made a very dramatic impression.

«My Gawd, what on earth must this poor woman've gone through?» sighed Vera, quite impressed.

«Life in Spain can't possibly be as dramatic as she's making it out to be!»

«I bet her husband left 'er for her best friend.»

«Or maybe the milk just boiled over.»

«What? D'ya think she's just actin' out scenes from the daily life of a Spanish housewife?»

«Might be.»

«No, it 'as to be something to do with strong emotions, like love and passion, or hate and pain.»

«Could be she just put the milk pan on the stove with love and passion and it boiled over anyway! The Spaniards've got a quite different temperament to us cool northern European types. They handle things different. Who knows? Maybe she just laddered her brand-new stockings?»

Then we had a long discussion about the connection between

the weather and the Spanish temperament and managed to survive another drag show. In any case we hadn't quite finished our drinks when they started playin' quite different tunes. For example, Brenda's most favourite song ever, «You're the One That I Want» from *Grease*, only the version by Hylda Baker and Arthur Mullard – she pisses herself every time she hears it!

All in all, folk music was very popular in Playa this season. We'd hardly set foot in *Na Und*, when they started playing *Mull of Kintyre*, *The Highland Lassies* and the *Pyrenean Mountain Goats* or something like that. I must say, being an inner city girl myself, these mountain folk all look the same to me. But somehow it all sounded very alpine and hilly and countrified to me. There was one song called *Madonna in the Eternal Ice* which really got me all tearful. I even made a point of learning the chorus, and it went something like this:

> *The walls of the glacier*
> *Glow red in the night*
> *Since that spring morning*
> *Her soul did take flight.*

You see this Madonna – no, not the one with the pointy boobs, another one! – had a terrible broken heart and was so distraught she went arse over tit on a glacier and fell down some crevasse! Of course nothing like that could happen to me in Soho!

The crowd in *Na Und* tends to be a bit on the older side, which is why a lot of the young queens call it 'Jurassic Park'.

Now, as you know, getting older is a bit of a touchy subject for us Marys. Recently I wanted to read up a bit on the *gay and grey* phenomenon so I went along to the local gay bookshop and discovered that there isn't a single book in the whole of England about the lives of older gay men. There are loads of books on coming out, about gays and astrology, queens in Hollywood, knitting and crocheting, and even gay cookbooks, but not a single volume about the experience of growing old gay. The whole subject is just completely ignored.

You're either young or you're dead, it seems!

I finally found a shocking line in Rosa von Praunheim's film *It's Not the Homosexual Who's Perverted* ... which summed it all up: «Growing old is at its cruelest for gays.»

Now if you want to believe all this rubbish, I certainly won't try and stop you shooting yourself at thirty-five. But if you're still not dead at fifty I suggest you get straight on the next plane to Playa and go to *Na Und*, coz they certainly know how to have a good time there! You certainly can't have as much fun as they do in *Na Und* when you're dead! But that's just by the by.

We'd hardly set foot in the place and Vera was off dancing a waltz with Champagne Shirley. She's this mature lady from Cambridge wot we met the year before. We called her that coz she always sat on the beach sipping champagne and often opened up the dunes in the morning, even though she was one of the last to leave the bars at night. She had a constitution like a brewery horse!

«If I'm here then I expect to at least have a decent dance,» she said, and spun Vera round and round till she came over all dizzy. Margot hardly ever missed a dance either. She's the proprietress of a beach bar on the promenade in Maspalomas, and a real woman by the way. We'd often pop in there last year if the first bell went off early and we fancied something decent to eat in between, or if we just couldn't face the walk home. You see it's ever so handy, from there you can get the bus back to Playa. Anyway, it's always really nice in there and Margot often comes into *Na Und*.

As we was sitting there having a lovely chat I suddenly noticed Martina standing next to me. She's a German OAP who now lives down in Playa and has found happiness there. Some bright spark gave her the name Martina coz she's often seen trolling about in very short tennis shorts. And she had some news for me that sent me right into a tizz!

«Yes, did you know zat your dreamboy Philippe has zplit up from zat Jemima? Vot d'ya say to zat zen?»

«Oh, then maybe I'll have a chance with him this year!» I suddenly let slip. «You could set us up if he comes in. Would you do that for me?»

«No, I never do such zings!» she said.

«Und anyvay Philippe izn't coming down ziss year.»

And so it is that joy and suffering, happiness and pain are always so close to each other! And then, just as we were setting off, this very young number came trolling in and quite unashamedly asked where the darkroom in *Na Und* was.

«There ain't one here. It'd go against cemetery rules!» answered someone behind me, just before he shovelled a whole handful of peanuts off the bar into 'is gob. Yes, that's how spiteful some of these girls can be!

After *Na Und* we set off to more mixed surroundings. First we popped in to see the Maharani in *Centre Stage*, but there was a whole football team of Scots going mental. All in kilts with nothing underneath! As they were all so jovial we decided to have a beer an' all.

When we finally got to the balcony over *Nestor's* at about half past one I thought Vera was having a heart attack. You see she'd just popped into *Tubos* for a pee and came running out in quite a state.

«You won't believe it. I've just seen a mirage!» she blurted out ever so het up.

«You 'ave? Wot then?»

«Denis Thatcher's sittin' in the back o' that club!»

«Wot? You must be mad. They'd never let 'im in 'ere. He'd drink the place dry and then there wouldn't be enough for us!»

«Look for yerself!»

So off we went. And sure enough, perched on a bar stool

right next to the dancefloor, there was Denis. Or at least this perfect double. I suppose he must have noticed me staring at him coz he started grinning back.

«Well, am I right?» asked Vera.

«They musta caught 'im shopliftin' at *Harrods* an' deported 'im!»

«D'ya mean Maggie?» this big butch bloke next to me started giggling.

«No, Denis. Or is Maggie here as well?»

«Nobody here calls him Denis. They all call him Maggie.»

«But he looks like Denis!»

«Precisely! That's why they all call him Maggie!»

Queen's logic, there's no beating it! This chap Oliver, that was the butch bloke's name, had been in Playa for almost three weeks and wasn't sure if he should be glad or sad that he was going home in two days.

«Well, me groin could take at least another three weeks,» he said, «but me mind couldn't stand it.»

«Wot?» exclaimed Vera. «Can't your mind take as much as your groin then?»

«The mind isn't quite as challenged here, is it?» he replied, and kept looking around the place like he was searching for something. «I'm meeting someone here you see. I met him on the beach today. A really nice guy. I hope he doesn't stand me up.»

«What's up with the washerwomen then? Shouldn't we be goin' over to *Claxx* soon?» I asked Vera as Oliver suddenly had a groaning fit.

«Heavens! He is goooorgeous!» he called out, and pointed at this tall blond number. «I've never seen him here before.»

«Really? He was standing right there last night an' all!» said Vera.

«What? Impossible! That can't be right. I'd've seen him.»

«Then he musta just fallen through your net then, luvvie,» I said.

In any case Oliver was totally gone. And the chap he found so attractive looked like Ken, the male Barbie doll. Tall, slim, kind of sporty and trendy with a right nice-looking kisser.

But just as Oli was giving him the full once over, along came the guy he'd been waiting for. He was pretty young, maybe under twenty, and he practically jumped into Oliver's lap he was so pleased to see him.

«The little'n isn't in love by any chance is he?» whispered Vera into my ear.

It certainly looked like it, though just as he tried to get up right close to him, Oli shoved him away abruptly.

«Have you been eating garlic? That stinks! No, I'm not having that!»

The boy looked as if he'd just been smacked in the face, stammered something about garlic being nothing unusual here in Playa, and anyway it was in pretty much all the food.

«Well you can just forget it. I'm not shagging a clove of garlic like you!» Oliver exclaimed, hard as nails, and kept looking over towards the Barbie doll. But she must have just gone to the loo or at any rate she'd disappeared in all the comings and goings, and Oliver got quite hysterical.

«How long have you been in Playa?» Vera asked the little chap to try and calm things down a bit.

«A week,» he said, and so we struck up a conversation with him coz Oli had completely disappeared in search of the Barbie doll.

Jamie was the little chap's name and he was on holiday with his parents in Playa. «Why is Oliver so mad at me?» he asked obviously very hurt. «That stuff about garlic is rubbish. I've only eaten perfectly normal food.»

«Well, you know ...» answered Vera the Wise, «some people just go a bit funny in the head here.»

«How d'ya mean?»

Well, you can imagine what happened next. How do you

explain to such a young thing like that what goes on in a gay club at two o'clock in the morning? At any rate, Vera took on the role of Mother Theresa while I set off into the crowds to have a good look round.

Except for one person from London who I'd managed to successfully avoid for years, there wasn't a soul about I really knew, despite taking a long diversion through *Mykonos*. There was this one rather strange couple I noticed though. Well, you really couldn't miss them. They were standing directly in front of the video screen. One of them, obviously a breeder, looked like Gloria Hunniford off the telly, and the other one looked like her daughter. They were just standing there in *Mykonos* obviously trying to have a conversation. It looked a bit strained, just like on Gloria's daytime talk show, but at the same time quite emotional: the mother was well-groomed, in her late forties probably, with an elegant and sporty drag and an expressive face, with a trendy highlighted hairdo. The daughter was a head taller, pretty skinny, in white jeans and a flapping Hawaiian shirt. A bit mousy-looking compared to the mother!

I was just about to shimmy past when suddenly Freddie Mercury's video *Who wants to live forever* came on. So of course I stopped dead in my tracks so I could sing along.

> *Who wants to live forever*
> *Who dares to live forever*
> *When love must die*

When I listen to it at home on the earphones I'm always deeply moved. And in *Mykonos* too of course, coz that's where life and love are lived out to their fullest. In any case, I picked up that this Gloria lookalike and her son were from Colchester and were on a sort of tour of exploration of the Gran Canaria gay scene together. They'd already been to *La Belle* and to *Café Marlene* I gathered.

By the time I got back to Vera and the rest of the gang it appeared that Oliver had finally landed the Barbie doll. She and Oliver and some other bloke were trying to make conversation.

«Well I hate cats! I simply can't stand' em!» said Oliver to the other bloke.

«Whyever not? They're such loving animals.»

«No they're not, they're two-faced.»

«What? There's enough pussies in this bar as it is!» I said.

«William here breeds cats,» Vera explained, and rolled her eyes somewhat annoyed. Then I caught on. Catwoman here was the Barbie doll's boyfriend and they came from Belgium.

«What are you doin' tonight then? Why don't we go back to my place for a drink. I've got a couple of bottles of sparkling wine, I think,» Oliver suddenly asked the Barbie doll, and I noticed he already had his knee between his legs!

«Sparkling wine?» she exclaimed, and must have been quite shocked as her eyebrows practically disappeared under her hairline. «That's a tart's drink. I only ever drink champagne!»

«I s'pose your cats only ever drink champagne too, eh?» enquired Oliver in a foul mood.

«No, they get Whiskas and water,» answered the Barbie doll as her boyfriend threw her a suggestive look. «And I think they must be quite hungry by now and need feeding.»

And with that the Belgian Beauties minced off leaving Oliver standing there all alone.

«Queens can be so cruel at times, it's just unbelievable!» he exclaimed, and suddenly turned back round to Jamie who'd been silently listening all the time, and started fiddling flirtatiously with his clothes. After a while he said: «Well, d'ya wanna hang around here any longer, or ...»

«Or what?» asked Jamie.

«You know your garlic breath really doesn't bother me all that much. I think I've got some chewing gum at home anyway.»

«Oh really? And did you bring your stamp collection along too?»

«What's the matter with you?»

«I'm pissed off coz I fell for a tart like you! I came all the way from San Agustin to meet you, and ...»

«Bye then girls,» called Vera, and off she swished and left me to listen to the argument all on my own! Mind you, I could see little Jamie's point of view.

«You're too clingy!» Oliver accused him. «We're not married, you know. I can do what I like. I don't need your permission, do I? My God, why do queens have to make everything so complicated?»

«D'ya think I want to be treated like a piece of meat in a supermarket? I s'pose you think being gay's just about fucking and nothing else, eh?»

«Oh, don't start getting all moralistic with me. You make me sick. Where did you get that crap from?»

*Dancing Queens* I can handle, but fighting bitches is one song I didn't want to listen to. But I don't blame Jamie. I mean, what would you have done in his place? Anyway, I buggered off to *Mykonos* as soon as I could, as I had no intention of spending the whole evening playing referee for them two!

«You'll never believe it!» cackled Vera the second I arrived. «I think I'm seeing things again.»

«Oh, what is it this time?»

«That Gloria Hunniford is sitting in the darkroom!»

«What? With a microphone?»

«No, with her son!»

«Now this I've got to see!»

Now the darkroom in *Mykonos* is right next to the bogs so you have to be really careful not to piss in it by accident if you're trying to have a look and see who's watching the porn while you're trying to have a slash. Well, Vera was right! On a bench in the darkroom was Gloria Hunniford with her daughter – all alone. The boy was looking up at the TV while his mother sat with her legs crossed, her elbows on her knees, and hand in front of her eyes. Every now and again she took a brief peek at the proceedings on the screen above her.

«Pretty brave of the chicken if you ask me,» said Vera.

«You must be joking. It don't look to me like he's got much say in the matter. Looks more like the old lady is doing the rounds of the gay scene to see exactly what's in store for her daughter!»

«Maybe she's just his best friend and they do everything together.»

«I mean really! Breeders in the darkroom! And female ones to boot! Are you mad? We really can't be having this. Come on, let's scare 'em off!»

«Oh, leave 'em. All the girls have fled the darkroom anyway.»

In fact, the only reason Vera didn't rush into action was coz she bumped into the Girl Guide Dog. She'd got herself a job in Playa and had been living on the island for a couple of months.

«What? Are you 'ere again? But I just saw you here in October, petal,» she cried in amazement. «How on earth can you afford it?

«I've no idea, love!» Vera began. «England's getting more and more expensive. I can't get by on the wages from me job with the Council. I've had to get a part-time job just to maintain a decent standard of living.»

«Really? What d'ya doo then, dearie?»

«Well, every evening after work I go scrubbing for three hours at the main post office. I started right at the bottom in the entrance hall. Terrible, I can tell you. The filth people drag in wiv'em, unbelievable! Especially in winter in slushy weather. You skid about for hours on that marble floor till you got it all nice an' shiny. But the other girls wot work there are right nice. And my Hindi's comin' on right nice, too!

And since last summer I've scrubbed me way up to the seventh floor. I just 'ave to flick through the corridors wi' a dry cloth up there and every third day I give it a damp rub over. Yeah, I get on right good there. And you see, the money I earn there I blow 'ere in Playa.»

Girl Guide Dog was obviously impressed and wanted to buy Vera a beer.

«Oh, that's very nice of you,» she said. «But let's go over to *Claxx*. They're bound to start hangin' out the washing soon.»

As we got there the waitress had just turned off that thumping 'one-size-fits-all' disco music that blares outta all the gay shoe boxes onto the gallery and sometimes makes you go all mushy in the head, and instead of that she'd put on some really fiery Spanish Sevillanas.

«Fabulous! It sounds like a bullfight is about to start any minute,» I announced all expectant. And as I took a closer look around in *Claxx* I noticed a whole crowd of Spanish queens standing near the entrance. They were cackling away quite happy to themselves, and then when the bullfighter music really got going some of them started jigging about and clapping their hands in rhythm to the music.

Now this kinda thing can be quite catching. So of course it didn't take long before Vera and me was having a good ol' clap along an' all. And suddenly there was this fabulous fun atmosphere. And then the washerwomen got going with their laundry.

Now I really don't know quite how I should describe this. Well, at first these two blokes'd rush at each other to the rhythm of the music as if they were going to crash into each other. Then, just before impact they suddenly stopped, took on a very proud, elevated stance and looked each other up and down with an incredibly arrogant expression as if they wanted to say: What d'ya want you silly cow?! And as they thrust their arms up into the air and held their heads bent down at an angle

to their armpits some of them made a disgusted face as if to say:
Oh my God, my deodorant's failed again!

And then, before they lifted their arms up again, they suddenly pinched their forefinger and thumb together like they were picking a peg out of a peg bag and then stretched up as if they were hanging up a piece of washing on a very high line. At any rate, they stretched their arms up over their heads as far as they would go and, except for the thumb and forefinger, splayed out all the other fingers. They held this very proud pose for a while, looked each other up and down again with that arrogant stare, and finally with short, rhythmical clapping they congratulated each other on hanging up another piece of washing on the line. And so with all that dancing they managed to peg out baskets and baskets of washing and luckily got closer and closer.

You see, to begin with they didn't physically touch each other at all. On the contrary, they moved towards each other in time to the music but then they kept drawing themselves up before each other like right stroppy bitches, shoved their hands on their hips, and glared at each other with scornful looks as if they wanted to say to each other: Do I need this? To lower myself to the level of a cheap tart like you? Not on your life, missus! But gradually things changed, as if they'd discovered some kind of attraction to each other, and after a while their dance became more lithe and they got physically closer. Finally they got so close to each other that the first tender gesture was hinted at, a gentle stroking of the partner's neck, almost as if he wanted to yank the head down for a passionate kiss. But before it could get that far they suddenly turned their backs again, strutted apart, and then started to approach and swoon around each other again.

«That looks absolutely fantastic,» even the somewhat odd Oliver had to admit. And I must say I thought so too. A real piece of Spanish folk dancing with a gay twist.

«I think it's much better than all those endless drag shows!» said Vera, quite excited. She'd already learnt how to clap her hands and make that typical staccato sound quite well. She just couldn't get the look right though! Her expression was far too friendly.

«Yes, I'll 'ave to practise that when I'm back 'ome in Manchester,» she said, and then suddenly shrieked: «Oh, I nearly forgot. I brought along a blank tape for them to record some o' this music for me. It really is sooo fabulous!» And off she shot to bring the waitress the tape. And ever since them hols Vera's been practising the Sevillana in Manchester. So if you ever happen to be trolling through the streets of Salford and you hear loud Spanish bullfighter music pounding out of some flat window then you know Vera's shoved all her chairs and tables to one side, rolled up the carpet, and is diligently practising. So you see, even a simple holiday in Playa can really change your life!

But this pegging out the washing didn't happen every night in *Claxx*. It just happened spontaneously or it didn't, depending on whether the Spanish girls were in the mood or not. Sometimes they just stood about and couldn't be bothered to get started. Or sometimes the waitress just didn't put on the right kind of music but said: «Sorry, the Brits want disco music!»

And so my first day's holiday drew to a close at four in the morning. It's really unbelievable how quickly you settle in in Playa you know. Somehow everything's exactly as you left it the year before, but somehow also completely different, if you see what I mean? On the beach too. I knew at least half of them in the first row, and you soon got to know the other half too.

The first day on the beach was spent flitting backwards and forwards from one sun lounger to another catching up on all the gossip of the last twelve months. Or with receiving guests at one's own sun lounger.

We noticed straight away that this year's latest fashion was dinky little miniature hand brushes. In all imaginable shapes and sizes. I even saw some with precious metal engravings. The girls used them for brushing the sand off the sun loungers and off their legs.

Now, I could go on about sand for hours, it's such a broad subject. The way some people spend hours brushing themselves off, you really cannot imagine. As soon as they come out of the water they squat on their sun loungers and wait for the sand on their feet to dry a bit and then brush it off really carefully before laying their feet gently one at a time on the sun lounger. But if somehow a bit of sand gets on it anyway they vigorously shake out the towels, trunks and any other bits of material that happen to be lying around. One queen even carried a placky bag full of water up from the sea and made herself a nice little flat front garden in front of her lounger. She kept watering it so the sand stayed moist and her feet didn't sink into the loose sand when she got up!

Some of them obviously had a regular sand phobia. Ralph from Bath was a right one. He spent all day on his sun lounger without making the slightest movement towards the sea.

«I can't believe that!» said John. «Why did 'e bother coming to Playa if 'e doesn't even go near the sea? Come on, let's just chuck him in t'water.» And as quick as a flash four lads got hold of him by the legs and arms and whisked him off towards the sea.

To our amazement Ralph didn't even struggle. I mean at the beginning he did cling onto his sun lounger like Kate Winslet to a piece of the Titanic and screamed «Mercy! Mercy!» But once they'd got him off and were carrying him over the sand he went remarkably quiet, didn't struggle at all and let himself get thrown into the water without any resistance.

«Why didn't you put up a fight?» I asked him when he'd fled back on tip-toes like some ship-wreck victim to a life-boat.

«Ugh! Then they'd've dropped me in the sand. That's much

worse than landing in the water!» he replied, and immediately set about rubbing all the grains of sand off his tootsies. He wasn't afraid of water at all, but quite simply hated the sand.

But you know there's a lot more of it about than you'd think. For example, there was these two Germans staying at the *Lenamar* under me and every evening one of them had this orgy of de-sanding! He put the beach bag on the balcony, got a damp cloth from the kitchen, and took all his bits 'n' pieces out of it one by one and wiped them clean of sand with his cloth. Then he turned the bag inside out, shook it out over the balcony like he was real mad at it, and then finally swept the balcony for half an hour with his broom.

«He must 'ave a pretty bad sand phobia,» I said to Vera after we'd watched this for a couple of days while sitting on my balcony enjoying the evening sun.

«I think he's more likely a house slave. Now I could really do wi' summat like that! It's a right pain in the arse always havin' to do everything yourself!»

But then, Vera is really ever so house-proud you know. Everything always had to be just so on her sun lounger. And then she'd look over to me and say: «You know Elvira, your bitta the beach looks like Steptoe's back yard. You really should get your pinny on an' clean up a bit you know!» But usually I only did that when I got in such a mess I couldn't find anything anymore! One time I found this enormous onion at the bottom of my beach bag that for some reason I'd been lugging back and forth to the beach for days!

I really don't know why my stuff always looks such a mess though. I've never been a real tidy housewife, but at times I could get right jealous when I saw how some girls had got all their bits 'n' pieces organised. First an elasticated cover over the sun lounger, then enormous brilliant white or cream-coloured sheets, pillows, small or large towels in between or on top or underneath – and all perfectly colour-coordinated and matching the swimming cozzie. I never manage that kinda stuff. I s'pose I'm just too dizzy?!

And I can't play football either! You see, shortly after Christmas a whole troop of lesbians appeared on the beach. They were so athletic they straightaway marked out a football field and goals and started kicking about.

There was five of us sitting on a lounger engaged in an intense discussion about the last episode of *Golden Girls* which unfortunately I'd missed when all of a sudden I got hit between the shoulders by this stray football.

«Ouch!» I shrieked, somewhat annoyed, and then all of a sudden one of the lesbians was standing there right in front of us and asked real friendly: «Hi boys, don't you wanna join in?»

Now what a ridiculous question! We could hardly believe she was referring to us! I mean, over the years you build yourself up a kind of identity in which things like playing football are just completely outside the normal realms of comprehension.

«What on earth makes you think that?» I was about to answer when I suddenly thought that that might leave a somewhat unmanly impression, and so I said, «Oh, no thanks. You play on your own. I'm sure you're much better at it than us anyway.» And so that's what they did, and we just sat and watched and clapped every now and again when one of the goalie girls flung herself at the ball with an amazing salmon-like leap.

But for our part we were often in the water. Especially when those wonderful swelling waves came in. And I'm afraid that wasn't as often as we'd have liked. But then the sea was packed. You see, these swelling waves were like someone'd tossed an enormous stone into the water a thousand miles away. Practically it's the same effect as when you throw a pebble into the vicar's pond – then you get these uniform circular waves that go out and out and out. The swelling waves, on an Atlantic scale, are kind of like that. They come in really evenly, lift you right up high, and then break with an enormous crash onto the beach.

Now when a thousand queens get whisked up into the air like this you can imagine what it sounds like! As if an air raid siren was going off somewhere!

But then when the wave had broken it was all quiet on the western front. Coz everyone had to find his way out of the foam and water and try to get to the surface to breathe. It was like the spin cycle in your Zanussi when one of them waves hit you. Then of course we had to have a head count to make sure all the girls had come up again. Some of them really had problems with them waves. Andrea from Wandsworth for example. She came up again all right, but then started splashing about and swimming around in circles as if she'd completely lost her orientation.

«Where's the coast?» she cried, «where's the beach? I'm blind! I've gone blind!» And after the next wave she was in a right state.

«What's the matter then?» I called over.

«I've lost me contacts! The waves've washed them out. I can't see a thing. Where's the coast?»

«Therrrre!» I screamed out, and pointed at the beach.

«Wherrre?»

Without her contact lenses she really was blind as a bat! When she finally got back onto dry land she quickly put in some fresh ones and was straight back off into the water.

«'Ave you stuck them in more firmly this time?»

«D'ya mean wi' superglue or what?»

«You could just use a Pritt Stick. That's waterproof an' all innit?»

I can't imagine how many contact lenses have been washed up on the gay beach at Playa. It'd probably be a profitable business to gather them all up and sell them off for recycling.

While these fab swelling waves usually came up when the

sun was shining and there wasn't any wind, other types of weather made for other types of waves, some of which could produce quite unpredictable currents. Especially when the tide was out. Now, a lot of people don't seem to realise that it can be pretty dangerous then. Particularly if you swim out far and on top of that aren't a very good swimmer. Believe me, every year a few go under! Simply coz they're too daft and think: Oh well, at home in the municipal baths I can swim all right. And I'm sure I'll be even better here in the sea. Them's the ones what wake up dead on the beach. And not in Playa, no, in Brazil, coz that's where the current takes them.

Two trolley dollies from Iberia were really lucky this Christmas that they was being watched from the beach by Chris and Ralph who usually sit in the front row. They saw how these girls' heads kept getting smaller and smaller, just coz the current was pulling them away off towards the lighthouse. And that's it for the next three thousand miles. The next thing after that is the beach in Brazil! In any case, Chris and Ralph are very good swimmers and they went after the Iberian girls, who were totally in a panic by then, and managed to calm them down enough that they gained enough confidence in their own strength. We all stood on the beach and watched to make sure all four of them didn't get washed away. Luckily they didn't. But it certainly took quite a while till they finally arrived, completely exhausted, back on the beach.

Best of all, you should do it like Vera did. First of all she just poked the tips of her toes into the water and cried out: «Ow it's cold! No, today it's particularly cold!» Then she went in a bit further. Up to her knees, until a small wave came. Then she fled back onto the beach. Sometimes she had really bad luck and the wave got her wet up to her arse. She managed to cope with that though, but held her arms right up high in the air and cried: «Oh, it's sooo cold! It's so terribly cold!» Then she went in a tiny bit further. Up to her hips. And then she started pointing to the waves with her index finger and talking to them. «You can do anything you like to me! Beat me, bite me, scratch me – but whatever you do, don't mess up my hair!» And it worked!

«No,» the waves answered, «your hair is like a goddess's tomb. It's sacred to us. It has never looked as healthy and shiny as today.» And so Vera usually came out of the water with dry hair. Even when the waves were quite strong, you see, there are always small wonders in the world what you can't comprehend.

We wouldn't've thought it possible though that anyone was daft enough to go out into the water on an air bed with a strong wind blowing out to sea. You see, you can very easily get blown out and by the time you've decided to part company with the air bed you can be pretty far out. But nevertheless, one afternoon this chap went in with his air bed while a pretty strong wind was blowing. He paddled around in the surf and we glanced up every now and again to keep an eye on him. But suddenly he was gone, and his boyfriend got right hysterical.

«Heavens, where the hell is he? He was there just now!»

«Has he come out of the water already?»

«No, then the air bed would be lying around here.»

«My God, maybe he's drifted out. And we didn't notice.»

In any case, things suddenly got right hectic. First off, we all had a good look to see if we could make out a head out there somewhere amongst the waves. We couldn't though. But when the sea's so choppy you can't see anything properly anyway.

«What on earth should we do?» they all cried helplessly, and rushed around on the beach looking out in all directions over the sea.

Then of course we informed the lifeguards and they got their dinky little walkie-talkies out and called up the coastguard. After a while they came trolling along in their little lifeboat and searched along our stretch of the beach. But found nothing!

But then all of a sudden the chap was there again. He had indeed drifted off, but not like we'd thought. In a second when he wasn't being watched he'd nipped outta the water, trotted down the beach, and then in a wide curve – so his boyfriend wouldn't see him – he'd marched off into Bongoland. With his air bed under his arm! There he had his fun!

I'm sure you can well imagine how majorly pissed off we all were at him. And his boyfriend in particular. He was outraged!

«You cheap whore you!» he screamed at him. «You've deceived me!»

«I have not! I was just 'aving a look round.»

«With an air bed under your arm? Tell that to your grandmother. 'Horing you was!»

Oh why am I even writing this? I'm sure you're perfectly familiar with this sort of marriage drama. In any case there's always at least two or three of them that cause a commotion in Playa every year.

«If I had a boyfriend I certainly wouldn't bring him here,» confessed this single chap from Brighton to me one day. He was sitting on my sun lounger having a chat and somehow wasn't really happy in Playa. And as I was chatting with him, Matthew from Northampton started snoring. Or at least he pretended to snore coz somehow he didn't seem to like this guy.

«Whyever not?» I asked quite surprised.

«When I've got a boyfriend I just don't go out on the scene.»

«D'ya think they'll steal him away from you or what?»

«Well, take a look at all these marriage crises here. I wouldn't expose my relationship to that risk.»

«Then I suggest you take a really good look around. There are loads of couples here – on the beach, in the bars, everywhere! It's only a small minority that have a problem with it. And marriage crises like that really are the exception.»

«Yes, but the temptation! It's lurking on every corner twenty-four hours a day.»

«Are you religious?»

«Nah, not me!»

«Well, how d'ya wanna live with your boyfriend then? D'ya just wanna hang around at home or what?»

«Nah, 'course not! My last boyfriend and me did lots together, went to the theatre, cinema. That kinda stuff.»

«Well, what kinda people did you spend time with? I mean, you still have friends and acquaintances don't you?»

«O' course. But they was all straight.»

«Oh! And they knew about you two?»

«Well, you really don't have to thrust your sexuality down everyone's throat do you?»

«Hmmm!»

«But now I've been single again for one an' a half years.»

«Is that why you're on holiday here then, to find a new boyfriend?»

«Could be, I s'pose.»

«'Course it could be. Though I still don't understand why you wouldn't come back here with your new boyfriend.»

«I just told you. I'm not into the scene. I just wouldn't wanna risk the relationship.»

Somehow I had this strong feeling that his next marriage crisis was already pre-programmed! It was lying dormant in the back of his head somewhere.

«Tell me then, what d'ya think's so terrible about the gay scene? Is it just the temptation you're afraid of?»

«Oh, I reckon the whole gay scene's just there so people can screw around all the time!»

«Really? You been screwing around a lot then have you?!» Matthew suddenly called over right bitchy, sitting himself up on his sun lounger. He hadn't been asleep at all but'd been earwigging!

«No, not *me*!» came the horrified answer. «But most of 'em are just out to get laid as often as they can. You can get used to that so quick. And then you're not capable of 'aving a proper relationship anymore.»

«Oh God!» cried Matthew. «I 'spose you think the gay scene's just there for fucking, eh? Well if you reduce being gay down to just that then I s'pose you must see it that way. But in reality it just isn't. Have a look at all the couples here on the beach. The majority of them come here coz they wanna meet friends, have a nice holiday, meet other nice people – first and foremost it's a question of socialising and not coz they all wanna fuck their brains out!» cried Matthew.

«And why are *you* here? You're single too aren't you?» asked the guy with just the merest smidgen of irony.

«Well, you'll never believe it, but my boyfriend's sitting at home at work! And he doesn't have the slightest problem with me 'aving sex with someone else here. He can do it at home an' all if I'm not there. As long as it's safe I don't have a problem with it at all. We've been together for ten years and we've never argued about sex. We have clear agreements which we stick to and still sometimes go out on the scene, have a beer and meet people.» Well, we'd stumbled into a major discussion on the nature of relationships. Even Claire Rayner could have learned a thing or two!

«Yeah, and in the scene the temptation is just too much,» said the Brighton boy again. «I just wouldn't wanna expose my relationship to it.»

«Oh, you just don't understand what I'm saying. You're the type of person who places small ads that say queens and scene types needn't bother! If you're too stuck up to cope with the scene, that's your problem. It's people like you that see the scene just as somewhere to fuck. You're so inhibited you think you can only have a real relationship outside of the scene. But that's simply not true!»

«I'm not at all inhibited!» insisted Miss Brighton.

«Oh heavens above!» Brenda would've cried if she'd been there. But she was stuck in La Palma, the silly cow. So I cried «Oh heavens above!» instead, and discreetly withdrew to the

169

Atlantic Ocean for a bit to cool off. But when I came back they were still bickering. About whether or not a relationship and the gay scene are compatible or not, and about temptation. Well I mean, it all starts with temptation don't it? Without temptation there'd be no boyfriend and no relationship. It really is always ever-present. You just have to know how to deal with it!

Luckily in the gay scene in Playa you really can't avoid temptation! Unless of course you run around with your eyes closed all the time or try and find Mr. Right in every guy you meet. But even then you have to experiment to see if you're a match or not, don't you?! In any case, there are so many ways of meeting men in Playa. Sometimes you don't even have to leave your own room!

That's what happened to Richard from East Anglia anyway. He'd rented an apartment near *La Sandia*. When he inspected it more closely he noticed there was a connecting door to the next apartment. Cosmopolitan and eager to meet people as queers tend to be, he tried it out to see if it was locked. And of course it was.

«Well, there's probably some ugly old troll staying there anyway,» he thought, and'd almost completely forgotten about the door when a couple of days later he was standing on the balcony and quite by chance peered round the corner to the next balcony and discovered a very interesting young gentleman relaxing in the evening sun with nothing more than a towel around his waist. And well, as these things go they took an instant liking to each other and – oh wonder of wonders – the door opened from the other side. And after that Richard always came to the beach with his connecting door companion.

Now, nothing practical like that ever happens to me, oh no! I got picked up on the kerb like some tart on the game! You see, I was trolling off home down the Tirajana from the *Yumbo Centre* at about half past three in the morning, minding my own business, when all of a sudden this white car stopped right in front of me.

«What's going on here?» I asked myself, and had a quick look at the driver. He didn't look at all bad – as far as I could see. But I wasn't about to just get into some stranger's car, I've read the highway code you know! So I carried on walking down the road, a bit slower though, and then the car moved on again and I had another look, and he had a good look and then, I'm not at all sure quite how it happened, but suddenly I was sitting in his banger and we was driving off to a quieter spot for a good rummage. But after we'd been rummaging around for a bit I decided it was a bit too cooped up in the car.

«Vengas a mi casa ...?» I asked him then, wot means in English something like: «He come with to my house?» and straight away he answered: «Sí, sí!»

Now, it was hardly a hundred metres away and Pepe parked the car on the Tirajana directly in front of *Pub Geminis*. Later on that turned out to have been a very good thing. So then we went up to my apartment and got straight down to the dirty business.

Now of course you always know better with hindsight, don't you? And that's why I always say: never get involved with married Spanish men. They're fabulous kissers, but apart from that they only want to do exactly what they do with their wives or whatever they are too ashamed to do coz the Pope's forbidden it. And of course condoms just don't even come into it!

I wasn't really happy till Pepe'd put his clothes back on and I'd closed the apartment door behind him. But as I'd just lit a ciggie, turned out the lights and glanced outta the living room window down the Tirajana to *Pub Geminis,* I saw Pepe get into his car and then shoot right back out again.

«He hasn't forgotten something, has he?» I thought, and fearing the worst rushed into the bedroom to see if his wedding ring was lying there amongst the debris. But there wasn't anything there. And as I was just going through in my mind all the places we'd been rummaging I remembered the stove in the kitchen. We'd been snogging in there for a while and I remembered hearing something clatter. In the middle of the frying pan I found an enormous bunch of keys that weighed a ton!

«He must be a prison warder!» was my first thought while I quickly pulled on some clothes. «But what are you gonna do now? The way he was guided by his willy there's no way he'd even find the right floor, let alone the apartment!»

So first of all I rushed out to the lift to see if he was on his way back up. He wasn't though. The lift wasn't showing any signs of life at all although I kept pressing the little button like an idiot. «Someone must have shut it off,» I thought.

So I shot down to the next floor and had a shufty through the corridors to see if anybody was wandering about down there. In a situation like this the corridors that are normally quite clearly laid out seem like an endless maze. «Hola! Hola!» I kept calling out quietly to at least give him a clue to where I was.

But the fourth floor was totally dead. As soon as I started pressing the lift button again I suddenly realised with a shock that I hadn't even got the keys to my apartment with me, but had just shot off without them!

«Oh God! I hope the wind hasn't blown the door shut!» I thought in total panic, and rushed on down to the third floor. But just as I shot around the corner I ran straight into Pepe! That gave me such a shock the keys flew outta me hand and clanked down the stairs.

«Madre mía,» he gasped, and groped for the keys while I, not losing a second, spun around and shot off back up the two flights of stairs like a woman possessed.

«Madre! Padre! Or whoever! Just let the bloody door be open!» I thought as I saw myself barefoot in knickers and a T-shirt trying to explain my predicament to the night porter and persuade him to come up and unlock my door! But «virtue is its own reward,» as they say and the wind hadn't blown my door shut. Was I a happy bunny?! I sat myself down, poured myself a stiff brandy, and watched Pepe get in his car and shoot off.

And what's the moral of the story? Exactly: quickies like that are just downright silly! Nothing like this would ever have happened to my girlfriend Lucy in the Sky, who in theory at least is very experienced in these matters. Which is why she advised me to get all the business done in the car instead of putting up with such unromantic complications in future. But sometimes romantic liaisons just do begin in a vehicle, even if it's a council bus!

That's what Bambi used to get each day from Playa to Maspalomas, and then walk along the water to the gay beach. She was this hairdresser from Dorset, and she was really called something else but coz she had these gorgeous brown eyes like that Bambi outta that Walt Disney film that's what we called her. Anyway, one day she came trolling down the beach in a foul mood.

«I must be doin' something wrong!» she moaned. «I was flirting with this bloke on the bus the whole time and he was flirting with me but I just didn't manage to strike up a conversation with him.»

«Were you sitting too far apart or what?» asked Frank from York.

«Not likely! The bus was totally full. We was standing next to each other. In the middle of the bus! Right by the exit!»

«Well, he coulda said something too.»

«He did!» cried Bambi.

«Well what then? I thought you said you didn't talk to him?»

«Well, it were like this,» said Bambi. «He got on the bus in *Campo de Golf*, stood right next to me, and started looking straight away. And when the bus went around a corner we kinda got thrown together and after that we kept smiling at each other. But then when the bus stopped one stop before the end of the line he just said: «Well, I have to get off here.» And I just got flustered and blurted out: «See you then, bye.»

«Good grief! And they always say the stupid ones are the best in bed!» exclaimed Frank.

«Well what was I s'posed to do then?»

«Why didn't you just get out too? I'm sure he was headed for the beach an' all.»

«Oh I always just go to pieces in situations like that and never get a word out. You always know better afterwards don't you? Maybe I'll find him somewhere,» said Bambi, and wandered off up and down the rows looking for him.

At times like that it's very useful to have a matchmaker at hand. The Lollipop Lady I shared my apartment with for a week met the man of her dreams like that. For two days she was swooning over Jason from Fulham and kept going on about how cute he was. And then Bert from Southampton decided to take pity on her.

«I can't take this any longer,» he said. «I'm goin' over to Jason and I'm gonna tell 'im.»

«For heaven's sake! You can't do that!» cried the Lollipop Lady in a fit of shame and turned scarlet.

«Whyever not? I know Jason and I'm sure he'll think you're nice too. But I'm not doing it for nuffink. You'll have to come up with a decent dowry!»

«O' course. What d'ya want then?»

«A big slice of cheesecake in *Café Wien*!» said Bert, and staggered off to arrange the wedding. Half an hour later the two new lovebirds were rolling around on a sun lounger in seventh heaven. And I was the one left standing coz I had to hang around and wait till they were done with their knocking sessions and vacated the apartment. I almost froze to death, I can tell you, when I had to sit around in *Café Marlene* till six thirty when they was finally done an' dusted!

Now usually it isn't a problem in Playa to take some gentleman with you into the rented accommodation. But not always, because some of the receptionists act like a Mother Superior in a brothel and get quite bitchy if they see two blokes going through at the same time. But all you really had to do was come up with a good story to get past them.

«Me visitor's just gonna help me peel the potatoes,» said Paul for example, and just held up a big bag of potatoes. And Colin always pretended to have sprained his ankle and let his lover practically carry him past reception and off to bed!

Now some people make such a racket with their sex sessions it's best if they have them out in the open and best of all miles from the nearest civilisation. But that's a particularly long story, and it actually started in the afternoon on the beach. You see all of a sudden the sky came over so dark, so quick that a regular panic broke out on the gay beach.

«Oh how awful, it's gonna pour down!» they screeched from all sides. And in no time at all most of them had pulled on their skirts and slipped into their shozzies convinced that a thousand queens can't all be wrong, and were marching off through Bongoland towards the *Riu Palace*.

«Wait a minute. Maybe the cloud'll clear in a bit,» somebody suggested. But of course no one was listening, coz as you know queens' hysterics are very catching! Within a couple of minutes the entire beach was de-queened. But hardly had we all fled into Bongoland and the sun was shining again.

«Well I'm going back to the beach,» said Vera, and rushed off back to the water. She never misses a chance to get brown and then wonders why she always has problems with immigration and people calling her the African Queen when she gets home!

«Oh, let's go to *Cita*,» said Robert. That was this GP from the north what always ran around in these ridiculously brief leather shorts, and must have brought at least six pairs along with him.

«Let's go to *Wien* first so Elvira can have her apple tart and then we'll see,» said Philip, and when we got there it was like a massive reunion of stranded refugees.

Richard and his connecting door number, the Sinister Sisters, Pom-pom Tom and Andrea had all downed their cake already and in the middle of the day had moved onto harder things. Now that can be catching too, and three hours later we was still sitting there sipping away. Especially Robert.

«Does she always knock it back like that?» I asked Philip. He'd known Robert the longest you see.

«Not really. I s'pose it must have something to do with the weather. Just look at that sky. It does look most odd.»

And as I peeked around the corner up at the sky I saw that a strange veil of dust seemed to hang in the air and the sun was shining kind of green through it. At the same time a warm dry wind had come up so that you had to keep rubbing your eyes.

«I've got to go'n rinse me lenses,» said Andrea. «They're burning like mad today.»

«Ya see! I told you so! It's a sirocco coming up.» Philip fore-told gloomily. «I know it. It'll be awful! A long drought'll come, and darkness will fall over the world and there'll be wailing and gnashing of teeth among men ...» I s'pose he'd just read *The Bible As History*.

«A long drought eh?» said Robert, and took another swig of his vodka and bitter lemon. «I don't care. As long as I've got me voddy I'll keep you damp, eh!» he slurred to no one in particular.

«What on earth is that doctress on about?» I asked Philip.

«Oh, I'm a wicked old woman! I can see it quite clearly in me crystal ball. A long drought'll come! Wailing 'n' gnashing of teeth ...» was all he answered again.

«We really should go'n get something to eat or we'll never get through the night,» I pointed out.

So that's just what we did. When I got to *La Sandia* at the staircase leading up to *El Chaco* there was Robert and Philip standing at these high tables sucking up the beer. In the meantime Robert had squeezed himself into a different pair of tight leather shorts, had put on a white shirt with the sleeves rolled up to go with it, and from his left shoulder over his chest down to his right hip he had on this brown leather strap. He looked so incredibly hot that these naff women at the next table couldn't peel their eyes off him.

«They're drippin' like a lorry-load o' gravel!» said Philip. «Come on, drink up. Let's go up to *El Chaco*!»

At that time in *El Chaco* though there weren't many naff women but a whole loada queens. And of course they all looked up from their plates like a building site full of gravel lorries!

«Hi girls!» shrieked the drunken doctress across the restaurant, and all of a sudden they all looked back down to their plates in embarrassed silence.

«Now pull yourself together!» hissed Philip. «Or you'll get a mouthfull!»

«Ooooh, will I reeeaaally?!» squeaked Robert back.

Luckily though dinner went off without any major derailments, and afterwards as we all trolled into *Nestor's* Vera was waiting for us with some news.

«A new bar's opened up 'ere in the *Yumbo*. It's one Planta down just around t'corner to the right. It's called *Contact*.» Now, I know curiosity killed the cat but we're no pussies, so as soon as we'd downed our coffee off we shot to investigate.

Well this place *Contact* really was the tiniest of shoe boxes and most unusual. It was right dark, and in one corner there was hardcore porn showing. On the walls there were loads of pictures of blokes getting a good beating, and a few characters were standing about at the bar. One of them, this older chap, had a big chrome ring through his nose which was connected to a hook on the bar by a long iron chain.

We'd just ordered our drinks when this young guy came flitting in, unchained the guy at the bar, and disappeared into a back room in a corner of the shoe box with him.

«Wot on earth's goin' on there?» asked Vera and got ears like rhubarb leaves. You know she's so nosy it's unbelievable. Not a thing gets past her that's going on in Playa. And what she don't know either don't exist, or it's just been invented the night before.

«Now this I've got to see!» she cried and off she went behind the curtain.

«Well, I expect that chap's getting 'is behind seen to,» assumed Philip, and gave Robert a slap on his leather shorts with the flat of his hand that really rang around the room. Seeing this, the landlord got this right excited expression, bent down and started rummaging under the bar. Seconds later he came up and put this enormous wooden spoon on the bar.

«Feel free, help youselves. I've got loadsa other utensils here an' all!» he said to us, and pointed to an entire arsenal of slapping instruments hanging up behind him.

«Oh, how practical,» cried Philip, and started waving the wooden spoon around. «Shall I cook you all something?»

«Oh, I dunno,» I murmured somewhat at a loss. «We've just eaten in *El Chaco*!»

Then Vera came scurrying back out of the back room. «Eeh, there's nowt that folk don't gerup to 'ere!» she announced quite prophetically, perched herself on a bar stool, and left us to stew in our curiosity.

«Well what then? D'we have to drag it out of you? Were they cooking something as well then or what?!»

«This is not a cookery class 'ere, this isn't!» she just said.

«O' course it ain't. What then?»

«Well, that older chappy, he was reliving a scene from 'is childhood.»

«Wot? How d'ya mean?»

«Yes, well, the other chap kept saying he'd never seen such a bad report ...»

«Well they can't possibly be reading reports in the darkroom, it's far too murky in there,» I said.

«That's just what I'm saying. They're playing a scene from 'is childhood. Didn't you ever get any E's on your school report and get your arse slapped for it?»

«Nah, my parents just didn't speak to me for days if I got a bad report.»

«Well you've probably got some other kinda complex from that no doubt. Anyway, that chap in the darkroom's bent over a trestle and the other guy's giving him what for on the arse wi' a leather strap.»

«Aha,» said Robert.

«Hmm,» I said.

«Funny,» said Philip.

«An' didn't he scream at all?» asked Robert.

«Yes, 'e did,» said Vera. «'The report isn't that bad.' He kept saying, 'I've only got three E's.'»

«I see,» said Robert. «A cheeky monkey and all then!»

«By the time I left though,» said Vera, «they'd softened him up a bit. He was crying 'I'll never get E's again! From now on I'll only get A's!' I think they're pretty much done now. 'Spect they'll be out in a sec.»

And so it was. As if nothing had happened, the two of them came wandering out of the darkroom all innocent-like, the young guy sat down to watch the porn and sipped his beer, and the older guy, who amazingly could still sit down, returned to his stool and carried on drinking too. He didn't hook his chain up to his nose again though. Obviously he'd been relieved of something!

I finished off my voddy and lemon and went home. At least every second day in Playa I have to be home by one a.m. Otherwise the next morning I end up looking like the queen on the

179

back of them new pound coins. You can't be out on the tiles every night now, can you? I mean after all, you shouldn't forget it's two shifts you have to do in Playa. First the one on the beach and then, after a short break, the evening one. I know some people that are so knackered after fourteen days in Playa they have to go home to recover. That's especially widespread among the Irish. You see, in Ireland there's as good as no scene at all coz that area's so dominated by the Pope and the God Squad. It's terrible you know! My good friend Nancy's been demanding for years that that old Polish nag be put out to grass – but nobody listens to a wise old housewife!

Now when I get home from all this turmoil I need a wee while to wind down. It's not as if I skip my night cream and go straight to bed. No, first I pour myself a nice glass of red wine and then I sit myself down and ponder for a while over everything that happened that day. And then – right at the end – comes the night cream. But on this particular night I could not get off coz the sirocco was raging away the whole time as if someone had plugged in an enormous hair dryer and was blowing hot air all around the place. And up on my fifth floor it was wailing and howling like in some haunted house.

When I staggered onto the balcony the next morning, still dog tired, to check up on the weather, Vera was already eagerly bustling about on hers. «Are you ready?» she called over. «Let's set off for t'beach right away.»

Now this was most suspicious coz normally she never gets going in the morning. She needs a mug of coffee and then another one and then she has to re-adjust her hair or sew a button on or potter about in her flat before she finally gets her arse into gear. By the time she's ready I've normally had at least one fit and set off to the beach on my own. This morning though she couldn't get off to the water fast enough.

And just as we were going through the arch of the *Riu Palace* she suddenly said: «I must just pop in for a pee,» and shot off into the hotel. The bogs in there are really most luxurious you know – compared to the cheap piss pots you have to put up with in the apartments anyway. But Vera took simply forever.

What on earth is she up to, her hair was perfectly all right, I thought, and wandered on ahead to that white terrace behind the hotel where the dunes begin.

When Vera finally came running out I could tell from a mile off that she was bursting with the latest gossip.

«Well Elvira,» she started, as soon as she was in earshot, «we really missed summat there! Last night all hell musta broke loose in them dunes! The entire west wing of *Riu Palace* was in uproar. The guests and waiters still haven't calmed down yet, coz of all the bestial racket what some folk was making in the dunes all night long.»

«That musta been the wind.»

«Oh come on. Someone was screaming like a stuck pig, and then there was this loud slapping like a whole class of naughty boys was getting seen to! The wind blew the sound of it straight into the west wing ... There musta bin some orgy going on in t'dunes!»

«Oh girl! You're imagination's getting the better of you again!»

At any rate, Vera just couldn't relax till she'd got to the bottom of it. Once she gets into Miss Marple mode there's no stopping her. And when we got to the sun loungers she sat there staring around at everyone, brooding away like some mother hen on her eggs.

«Hey Elvira, d'ya notice anything different here today?» she suddenly asked after about an hour.

«No. Just that that gorgeous Spanish guy that's usually in the first row with 'is sister ain't here today.»

«And nothing else?»

«Nah!»

181

«Well, just take a look at Robert. He always goes into the water naked. And today he's not taking off 'is cozzie at all. Funny that, innit?»

«Come on, I don't have to explain to you what the girls are like. One day they're into bare bots and the next they're into cozzies.»

«No, there must be another reason. He's not lying on 'is back at all today either. He's only lying on 'is front.»

«Well maybe he just wants to get 'is back browner. You're always saying to me: Elvira, you should lie on your tummy for a bit. Your back's as pale as a nun's tits! Aren't you?»

And just as Vera was bustling about like Margaret Rutherford, Philip came trolling over. «Well? Was I right or what? I may be a wicked old woman, but me crystal ball never tells no lies. Wailing 'n' gnashing of teeth ...»

«Ya see!» Vera turned to me triumphantly.

«Come on, did the sirocco blow your brains out or wot? I've never 'eard such a loada bollocks!»

«It were in t'dunes weren't it?» said Vera straight out, and Philip nodded.

«Robert's arse looks a right state. All red 'n' blue and covered in weals 'n' bruises. He must've been gagging for it. He couldn't get enough.»

«Yeah, and in t'west wing of *Riu Palace* ...»

Of course Philip didn't know what Vera knew, and slowly I was putting two and two together as well. You see, Robert had stayed quite a bit longer in that strange cooking studio the night before and it must have turned him on so much that he decided to get himself something striking too! And because that kind of sex makes so much noise they went off to the dunes – out of consideration, they thought! In a taxi!

You see! In Playa every Jack finds his Jill! You just have to know what you want.

Vera of course couldn't give it a rest though till she'd found out exactly who had beaten the shit out of Robert. That evening in *Nestor's* she was still Marple-ing away.

«Look Elvira. Robert keeps looking over at that Darren over there. D'ya think it was him?»

«Nah, if it'd been him he'd have at least said hello when he came in. He didn't though.»

«Oh come on. Where've you been the last twenty years? It's nothing unusual for queers who shagged each other stupid the night before not to know each other the next day. No. No, I think it were Darren. You see, he's hitched up wi' this baker woman, and she had to go to bed at ten o'clock last night coz she had to get up at four this morning to bake, and so ...»

«Exactly,» interrupted Philip. «After all, me crystal ball did go on about a long drought. That fits Darren exactly. He's at least six three, and he's pretty dry if you ask me?!»

«And what about the sirocco?» I asked.

«Wot? Haven't you noticed? That wasn't a sirocco at all but just a *calima*. It stops blowing after a couple of days. No, the long drought was definitely a reference to Darren!»

Well, what can you say to that? There isn't anything that folk don't get up to here, and anyway queens do all tend to live in their own little worlds, don't they?! That's what makes the whole thing so gay and diverse and never ceases to amaze you and teach you something new.

Now take for example my good girlfriend Lucy in the Sky. In the whole two weeks she was in Playa she only went out on the scene once. And that was to *Nestor's*. And then she spent all her time doing isometric exercises.

Maybe you're familiar with this form of exercise? Most queens that go to the gym are, but just in case I'll write them down so you can practise them if you want. Well, get yourself a chair and first of all sit yourself down on it comfortably on the front of the seat. Let your arms hang down loosely to the left and right. Then stretch out your left foot as far forward as you can, but be sure to keep the tip of your shoe firmly on the ground. Now if you've already got cramp in your calves by now it just shows how much more you need to relax. As a beginner it's OK if you pull your foot in a bit nearer to your body. Then lift up your right leg a bit and slide it carefully over the left, placing your right foot on the ground to the left of the left one. Then press your left foot down so firmly that it looks as elegant as possible. But be careful, the right foot must remain on the ground too! So, and now take your right arm and lay it, with an open palm upwards on your left knee – your wrist should be lying exactly on the left half of the right knee. Finally, with a smooth semi-circular movement, put your left hand in the open right one.

Now you're probably sitting there as crooked as a question mark, so we'll come to the upper body. Give your back a shove, just above the hips, so that you're sitting up almost straight. Now pull your shoulders back and thrust your chest out forward so that you're sitting up perfectly straight. Now don't let your head hang down, that looks far too sloppy, but hold it up so that your spine and neck form a perfect straight line. By the way, you should never come into contact with the back of the chair. Never!

And now we come to the grand finale: Smile, smile, smile! Completely relaxed and open to the world.

Now does this exercise sound at all familiar?

«You're sitting like Princess Anne at some stately reception again!» said Miss Diamond, that's Lucy's other half, and gave her a good shove. But that didn't bother Lucy in the slightest. She just carried on with her exercise.

I mean, in a way it is just like a reception isn't it, when you sit around in gay bars. You're seeing and want to be seen, so why shouldn't you present yourself like a real queen? «Everybody wants to be perfect,» my girlfriend Paula always says.

But the French are definitely the best at it. Pay attention

to how they greet each other. It's just superb! Shortly before Christmas for example, a group of at least half a dozen French girls was sitting having coffee in *Wien* and was parleying away happily to each other when a seventh and an eighth, obviously just flown in, came and joined them.

With cries of the most joyous surprise all six of them got up at the same time – still holding their coffee cups or cake forks or whatever – and that amazing kissing ceremony got underway: first the left cheek, smooch, and then the right, and then in the middle or sometimes on the left again. And that all the way round the table or, with stretched bodies and long necks, right across the table. Quite delicious!

Now just calculate for a minute exactly how many kisses were exchanged there. Thirty-six, all in one go! I grabbed hold of my coffee cup, poked out my little finger, and just joined in the ceremony simply to get a bit of that cosmopolitan feeling. But what can I say? They didn't even notice that a little Elvira had sneaked her way in – they were so taken up with it. That's just the way it is in Playa!

But after four weeks you do kind of look forward to getting home.

This time my plane left at a very gay-friendly hour. Three thirty in the afternoon. That way I could have a fabulous last night out and the next day still lie in and have plenty of time to pack my cases.

While I was waiting for my plane at the airport and gazing down onto the gangway where all the fresh new arrivals come through, I recognised quite a few old friends.

«Coo-ey!» I naturally called down.

«Coo-ey!» they answered. «Are you flying home already?»

«Yeah, 'fraid I've got to!»

«Then I wish you a safe landing in London.»

«Thanks, and you all have a fabulous holiday. Maybe we'll see each other again next year.»

«When are you coming back again?»
«I dunno! But definitely next December.»
«Well bye then. See you next time.»

To do 1 to 2 weeks before trip:

- ☐ Money for hols
    - ☐ Order travellers cheques
    - ☐ Order foreign currency
- ☐ Deposit rocks and valuables in bank safe
- ☐ Make sure important stuff at work is covered
- ☐ Inform secretary
- ☐ Have car checked over at garage
- ☐ Organise care of house plants
- ☐ Organise travel and luggage insurance
- ☐ Make any necessary doctor or dentist appointments (get pill prescription in advance)
- ☐ Foreign health insurance
- ☐ Get necessary vaccines
- ☐ Check that cases and that special bag are OK
- ☐ Addresses for postcards
- ☐ Organise holiday quarters for all pets
- ☐ Inform security service if applicable
- ☐ Re-direct newspaper or magazine subscriptions
- ☐ Make sure answering machine is fully operational
- ☐ Make sure house insurance is adequate and paid up to date
- ☐ Pay any outstanding bills
    - ☐ Electricity  ☐ Gas  ☐ Water
    - ☐ Phone  ☐ TV licence

To do a couple of days before hols:

- ☐ Use up any leftover groceries  ☐ Cancel the milk
- ☐ Empty vases  ☐ Fill out advance lottery tickets

Packing your case

- ☐ Toiletries, shower gel, shampoo and towels
- ☐ Umbrella  ☐ Aspirin, toothbrush, floss
- ☐ Sunglasses, spare glasses / contacts if applicable
- ☐ Suncreams, after-sun  ☐ Medications

- ☐ Mirror, manicure set, comb ☐ Safety pins
- ☐ Shoe cleaning stuff ☐ Spare shoe laces
- ☐ Tissues ☐ Sewing set, scissors, spare buttons
- ☐ Cigarettes and lighter ☐ Alarm clock ☐ Torch
- ☐ Penknife ☐ Compass ☐ Mobile phone
- ☐ Laundry bag and washing powder ☐ Short washing line and pegs ☐ Pen ☐ Notebook ☐ Diary
- ☐ Something to read ☐ Crosswords ☐ Games
- ☐ Playing cards ☐ Radio ☐ Camera and film
- ☐ Musical instrument ☐ Thermos flask ☐ Tea bags
- ☐ Dish cloths ☐ Bottle and can opener

## Special Items for Ladies

- ☐ Dresses (day, evening and cocktail) ☐ Suits
- ☐ Skirts ☐ Blouses ☐ Pullovers ☐ Cardigans
- ☐ Knickers ☐ Stockings and socks ☐ Bras
- ☐ Long trousers ☐ Shorts ☐ Jewellery ☐ Scarves
- ☐ Swimming cozzy ☐ Bath robe ☐ Pyjamas or nightshirt ☐ Shoes, sandals, slippers, trainers
- ☐ Tissues ☐ Cotton wool ☐ Curling tongs
- ☐ Raincoat ☐ Gloves

## Cosmetics

- ☐ Make up ☐ Face powder ☐ Lipstick ☐ Fragrance
- ☐ Nail polish and remover ☐ Hair spray, gel, mousse
- ☐ Curlers ☐ Deodorant

## Special Items for Gentlemen

- ☐ Suits ☐ Shirts ☐ Underwear ☐ Socks
- ☐ Pyjamas or nightshirt ☐ Belts, braces ☐ Ties
- ☐ Scarves ☐ Gloves ☐ Cuff links ☐ Dressing gown
- ☐ Shaving things ☐ Swimming trunks ☐ Tracksuit
- ☐ Shorts ☐ Shoes, slippers, sandals, ☐ Raincoat

Special Items for Queens
(See also Special Items for Ladies & Gentlemen)

☐ Alka-Seltzer  ☐ Condoms  ☐ Lube ☐ Extra tissues  ☐ Hair
  dryer ☐ Poppers☐ Dildos
☐ Other toys ☐ Chaps and other leather gadgets
☐ Jockstraps ☐ Cuddly toys  ☐ Gay guides
☐ Elvira in Gran Canaria    ☐ Walkman & CDs


To do the day you leave

☐ Take pets to pet-sitter
☐ Empty the fridge, defrost it and leave door open
☐ Pull all plugs out of sockets (TV etc.)
☐ Give your holiday address to neighbours, friends and relatives
☐ Give neighbours spare house key
☐ Pack provisions for the journey
☐ Aspirin ☐ Fruit ☐ Biscuits ☐ Nuts
☐ Chocolate ☐ Drinks ☐ Sweeties
☐ Close all windows and doors    ☐ Draw the curtains
☐ Make sure you've got all necessary papers
☐ Passport  ☐ Driver's licence ☐ Tickets
☐ Credit cards ☐ Cheque card
☐ Reservations for hotel, car rental etc.
☐ Turn off gas and water    ☐ Lock the garage


☐ Carefully lock the front door

Nice to read in holidays

and on the beach

ISBN: 978-3-928983-92-1

The queer version of Oscar Wildes famous play,
plotted as a graphic novel by the
Belgian artist Tom Bouden.

www.maennerschwarm.de

# Ralf König

## Germany's internationally acclaimed gay comic artist

The story of Konrad and Paul – and the spanish beefcake Ramon.

ISBN
978-3-928983-51-8

The story of two dogs and their gay masters.

ISBN
978-3-935596-74-9

www.maennerschwarm.de